WE SPEAK THROUGH THE MOUNTAIN

ALSO BY PREMEE MOHAMED

IN THIS SERIES

The Annual Migration of Clouds

THE VOID TRILOGY

Beneath the Rising
A Broken Darkness
The Void Ascendant

COLLECTIONS

No One Will Come Back for Us and Other Stories

NOVELLAS

The Butcher of the Forest
The Siege of Burning Grass
No One Will Come Back for Us
And What Can We Offer You Tonight
These Lifeless Things
The Apple-Tree Throne

PREMEE MOHAMED

WE SPEAK THROUGH THE MOUNTAIN

Copyright © Premee Mohamed, 2024

Published by ECW Press
665 Gerrard Street East
Toronto, Ontario, Canada M4M 1Y2
416-694-3348 / info@ecwpress.com

All rights reserved. No part of this publication
may be reproduced, stored in a retrieval system,
or transmitted in any form by any process —
electronic, mechanical, photocopying, recording, or
otherwise — without the prior written permission
of the copyright owners and ECW Press. The
scanning, uploading, and distribution of this book
via the Internet or via any other means without the
permission of the publisher is illegal and punishable
by law. Please purchase only authorized electronic
editions, and do not participate in or encourage
electronic piracy of copyrighted materials. Your
support of the author's rights is appreciated.

Editor for the Press: Jen R. Albert
Cover and interior illustrations: Veronica Park
Cover design: Jessica Albert

This is a work of fiction. Names, characters,
places, and incidents either are the
product of the author's imagination or
are used fictitiously, and any resemblance
to actual persons, living or dead, business
establishments, events, or locales is entirely
coincidental.

Library and Archives Canada Cataloguing
in Publication

Title: We speak through the mountain /
Premee Mohamed.

Names: Mohamed, Premee, author.

Description: Series statement: The annual
migration of clouds ; 2

Identifiers: Canadiana (print) 20230620760 |
Canadiana (ebook) 20230620809

ISBN 978-1-77041-733-5 (softcover)
ISBN 978-1-77852-264-2 (ePub)
ISBN 978-1-77852-265-9 (PDF)

Subjects: LCGFT: Dystopian fiction. |
LCGFT: Novels.

Classification: LCC PS8626.O44735 W42
2024 | DDC C813/.6—dc23

This book is funded in part by the Government of Canada. *Ce livre est financé en partie par le
gouvernement du Canada.* We acknowledge the support of the Canada Council for the Arts. *Nous
remercions le Conseil des arts du Canada de son soutien.* We acknowledge the funding support of the
Ontario Arts Council (OAC), an agency of the Government of Ontario. We also acknowledge
the support of the Government of Ontario through the Ontario Book Publishing Tax Credit,
and through Ontario Creates. We acknowledge the support of the Province of Alberta through
Alberta Foundation for the Arts.

PRINTED AND BOUND IN CANADA   PRINTING: FRIESENS   5 4 3 2 1

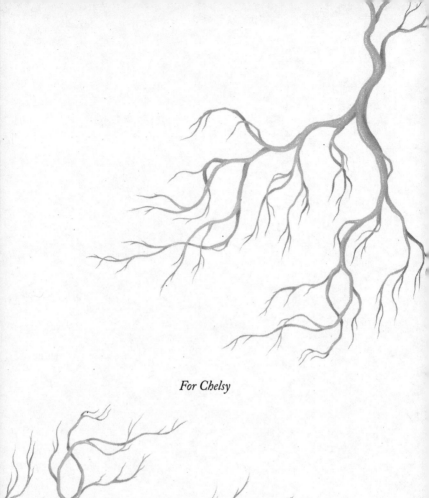

For Chelsy

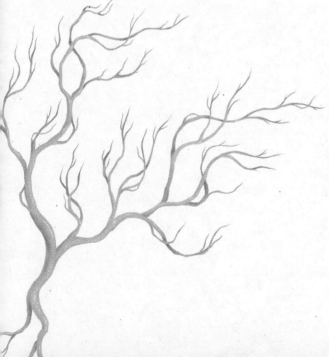

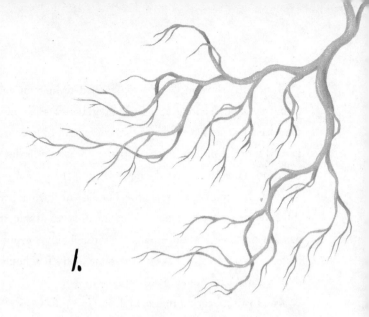

1.

We tell the kids, *Never travel alone*. We tell them, *Go where you like. But don't go alone*. We start teaching it in preschool, before we expect them to learn anything else. This is the first thing we want them to take in. And now this.

I am alone. More alone than I have ever been in my life and simultaneously not alone. I travel with the adversary. I carry the infection like a weight and a conscience.

How long have I been climbing tonight? Four hours, five? I wish for numbness. Instead my entire body prickles with perception, as if I am one giant nerve ending, slithering up and up through the rocks. No snow falls but the wind grates and burns. I had this idea

(one of us had this idea)

that ascending would bring me to safety, because it is hard to pursue someone who has the higher ground. I hope I'm right.

I stopped shivering long ago, stopped feeling my bike chafe my shoulder long ago. In the darkness I sense more than see a plateau screened by a thin copse of dead larch, and I crawl into the meagre shelter, luxurious because it is out of the wind. Time to stop for the day.

Tonight I must risk a small fire. For days my life has been this constant patter of mental calculation: this versus that, the dangers of doing and not-doing, the virtually imperceptible increase in safety or not . . . all the same, every few hours I think clearly, I am going to die out here.

No, I won't. I can't. I refuse. I refuse.

I'm going to die.

I can't. I am a multitude.

Firelight dances on the grey stone around me, on the corrugated bark of the trees. I drink in its warmth, sit as close as I can, hungry for heat. It's funny because I'm feverish and yet I still want more heat. Yes, I know I am. Mom always said you can't feel a fever in yourself but I know. I feel.

I empty half of my canteen into my all-purpose metal mug so I can stew some dried pork and mushrooms. Usually my big meal is breakfast — fuelling strength to climb. But I threw up my breakfast this morning and climbed anyway. I'm lucid enough to know that was *bad*. And enough to watch the fire and to watch myself. Luckily.

Since we reached the mountains, the adversary wouldn't let me climb down into the lakes and puddles to get water. Just would not. Sometimes it let me refill my canteen from a waterfall or a stream, even though these were few and far between compared to the still waters. I began rationally, trying to explain to it that those ponds and lakes were hardly algae-scummed deathtraps, and what if I ran out of water waiting for the next stream? Then I lost my temper. I screamed at it. I accused it of both homicide and suicide. When I left home, I thought we were coming to some kind of rapprochement; now I hate it more than I've ever hated anything in my life.

"Why?" says the dead boy across the fire. "*It* didn't kill me."

"Nobody asked you," I tell him. He's been showing up more often at night. Voice mushy through his crushed skull, scant bloodied blond hair sticking up like porcupine quills. "You hate what you want to hate, and I'll hate what I want to hate."

It's okay. I know he's dead. I know he died in the boar hunt that I was in, my first hunt, the one I thought would let me leave home with a clear conscience — and I know the deaths and maimings weren't my fault, but you'd never know it from the way he talks. He comes and — there he goes. Now it is just the flames again. I wait for bubbles to form in my mug perched on the embers. You have to make sure it's boiling for at least a couple of minutes to kill off whatever might be in there.

That's the thing about being alone. That's *why* we tell the kids not to go anywhere alone. Because if something happens, no one can help you. And no one can go for help. And no one will know.

What am I doing, for Christ's sake. Why am I here. What was I thinking . . .

"You wanted an adventure," my best friend says just behind my left shoulder, as if the stone itself were speaking. I feel it thrum against my back.

I don't turn. "That wasn't it."

"Yes it was. You never had one at home and you thought: I want to be like the kids in the books. I want my own adventure."

"Shut up."

"How's it going, anyway? *Is* it like the books?"

I'm watching my dinner. Tiny bits of foam are appearing on the flame side; I wrap my hand in the end of my scarf and rotate the mug so it heats evenly. "Yesterday I saw . . . or maybe it was the day before. You weren't there. I was following my map and I stopped to look down at how much distance I had covered, at the highway down there — and for just a second I was so proud of myself. Because it was so far below me, because the view was so beautiful. And I saw . . . people. Ten or twelve people. I was trying to think of what was odd about them, and then I saw . . . it was all men. Walking along quietly. In a line. And in the middle of the line there was a cart on two wheels, like one of our handcarts but bigger — being pulled by two women. Naked. Bloody. And I stopped moving. I thought: What if I could become part of the rock. I thought if they saw me . . . you already know what was in the cart. You already know it was a cage. I don't need to tell you that."

Henryk's voice says, "Maybe you didn't see it, Reid."

"Maybe."

"Because you're hallucinating a lot now, you know."

"I know."

The men didn't see me. I waited for a full hour, sweating in motionless silence, feeling every particle of the stone under my fingertips where I had flattened myself to the ground. I hoped I would hear them if they circled around to get me. No one came. I went on. I felt like something had broken irreparably inside my head and I vowed not to think about it again.

I fish my mug out of the fire and eat, pausing now and then to allow a tremor to run through my hands. No sense fighting it; have to let it pass.

"Funny you shouldn't object to this," I tell the adversary, which cannot speak. "You know. Letting me eat mushrooms. Isn't that something like cannibalism? Close enough?"

Henryk's not wrong about the hallucinations, anyway. I've been talking to him, Gabriel, Nadiya, Aldous Wong, the adversary. I hear my mother. I hear my father. I talk back to the birds that shout their alarm calls as I pass. Earlier I could stop myself. Now I can't.

The thing is, I've gone too far to get back on my own, and realistically I can only go forward. The steamcart took me to the edge of Calgary — the fastest I've ever moved in my life, initially terrifying but good preparation for when I eventually got going on my bike — and I've been on my own from there, waiting for my tracker to go off at the zone marker. I followed every direction the university sent me in my acceptance letter.

I can't go home; it can't exist for me any more. I mustn't think of my past. And while I am here I don't dare think of the future, either. I am trapped in a small, endless now of darkness and pain and fever and hunger.

Near my head, a whiskeyjack cries out, a startled yelp, then darts across my clearing, for a moment gathering all the light of the flames as if it is a carelessly thrown shard of glass. I've never heard one at night before. I stare after it, stupefied in the restored silence. What ... why ...

When the rocks begin to patter around me, I still haven't come to any conclusions, and it's my body that rises to fight, left hand a fist, right holding my knife, the disease darkening suddenly on my exposed skin like ink, as if it too has gotten up and could simply burst through my skin in a spray of black and blue. For terrible moments we hang in the balance, something inside urging, *Don't, don't. Lie down and let it happen*, and the rest of me shouting, *Don't touch me, don't come near me, and if you touch my bike I'll fucking kill you.*

Lights fill my vision, but I'm ready for that, and I lunge — freeze — feel the disease lock my muscles in stasis, able only to snarl like a dog at the end of a leash, held in abeyance by some greater weight hauling back on the other end. Not now! Let go! Let me fight! I cannot make sense of the noises I hear, they dance on the edge of meaning but never quite reach it before dissolving into garbled syllables again.

My knife rebounds from something hard, then is snatched from my hand. Someone kicks out my fire. I release a cry, a brute and wordless sound echoing harshly from the rocks. Fire was my other weapon. Counting on it for animals. These are no animals. Are they. Unless up here they speak.

Something slaps the side of my neck, leaving a strange, cold burn, and my eyes begin to slide closed. Someone else pulls my tracker necklace up and over my head, the little orb sparkling past my face. My last thought as I am swarmed is how best, without a knife, I can solve the problem of my own existence if what I greatly feared has come to pass. If I didn't outpace that gruesome caravan I saw; if they saw me and hungered for me and these are their hands on me.

Let me tell you. Let me. What we teach the kids if the worst happens. What we tell them about . . . what we . . . because we love them.

2.

I wake gradually, aware at first only that I am coming out of sleep, then walking dazed through the levels and levels and levels of it like a labyrinth. Warmth and dim light, a smell of bad moonshine, something else under it — harsh to the nose. Distant voices. Under my hands, fabric; under my head, something hard but yielding: plastic. That's familiar at least.

There's a ceiling above me and even though that's a good sign I still squeeze my eyes shut and outwait a huge wave of panic, gritting my teeth until it becomes ordinary worry, then confusion, suspicion, and resignation. I am used to waiting things out.

"Reid? How are you feeling?"

The voice gives me something to focus on and the rest of the space snaps into clarity: a curtainless window set in a white wall, a white door with no handle, a grey blanket covering my right leg and tucked under my left, which is bandaged and elevated on a kind of lacy plastic scaffolding.

The owner of the voice is pale, with thinning dark hair and a short beard, dressed in what I guess are the clothes of technological utopia — a seamless blue shirt, lighter blue pants, and a wristwatch with a narrow black strap. I admit I had been imagining something more futuristic. Silver jumpsuits, maybe.

Behind him is someone who has not yet spoken — a tall, broad-shouldered woman with swept-back silvery hair and the calm expression, as well as the hot golden eyes, of a bird of prey. She is dressed in white so that for a second I wonder if her plan was to blend into the wall, as if I would not see her.

How *am* I feeling? Aside from those animal parts of the body informing me I need to eat and pee and stretch, cautiously optimistic: the fever is gone, or much reduced, and I don't feel entirely nuts any more.

"I'm fine," I tell him. "How long did I have that patch on me?"

He chuckles, a little chagrined, letting me score the point. "I'm Dr. Gibson and yes, you're in the infirmary at Howse. The patch was on you for as long as was needed. Looks like you had a rough time before that, hmm? Getting here?"

Getting here. "Where's my bike?"

"We put it in your room. It's safe. It's *safe*, please don't stand up. What happened here, if you don't mind my asking?"

He's pointing at my leg with a pen. We both look at it as if we expect it to do something interesting: speak, change colour, blow up.

"Animal bite."

"Before or after you left home?"

"Before."

I'm half-listening as he tells me the story of my ankle because I am telling the same story at the same time, from the other side. I fell on the forest floor and (there was dirt under the skin that) the sow snatched me in her jaws because (wounds became infected and the bacteria mobilized into your) we were the enemy, knowing damn well (surprised; you were walking on a hairline) how fragile and small a human is compared to a pig (could have died) and I could have died.

"We cleaned it out and re-sutured it," he concludes, "and the IV antibiotics are knocking back the infection. The fracture will resolve in a few weeks now that you can keep your full weight off it. It wasn't very wise to travel with it in that shape. You must have been in a lot of pain."

"It just felt hot and kind of numb. I knew something was wrong, but . . ." And here I cannot tell him of the early days of the journey astride my precious, resurrected-from-extinction bike, propelling it with my feet till I learned how to pedal and balance properly, the moments of joy and freedom in between the hours of terror and loneliness, how I could not even hear the alarm bells ringing in my bloodstream over the crushing sensation of the mountains first looming over me then closing around me like jaws, how the outer fear was so much greater than the inner, and how my disease did not want me to move one more step every morning, *not one more*, and how I had to fight it till I thought we would both die in the effort.

I glance up at the woman in white, who's smiling as if she just heard my entire internal monologue, and she says, "I'm Dr. Cardinal, Reid. I'm the president of the university."

"Oh. Pleased to meet you. Do you . . . do this for every new student?"

"No, no. I simply heard you came here after, as the good doctor says, a rough time, and I wanted to say in person — I admire your tenacity and determination to reach us. That's very much in the Howse spirit. Welcome! I hope you'll soon forget the trip here and focus on more pleasant things."

"Uh . . . thank you."

I wait for her to leave after this speech, but she simply folds her arms across her chest and watches me. The president of the university. Surely she has better things to do. I swallow nervously and glance at Dr. Gibson. "Can I see outside?"

"Oh, sure."

The plastic scaffold looks delicate but is meant to be used as a kind of shoe; I am allowed to limp cautiously around the room, clutching my silky white gown, with the doctor offering his arm in case I fall. Window first. If nothing else, I must see the hemisphere that encloses the dome, which I have been imagining all my life whether I admitted it to myself or not. I picture diamonds, gems, impenetrable geometry set with all the care and dedication of Back Then's engineering to form an unbreakable barrier no different from the photos of the Mars colonies.

The buildings are subtle, blending precisely into the stone of the mountain, even though I know they can't be made of stone — they just *can't* — it is too disappointing to think of these people, the *dome* people, building out of stone like cavemen.

Cardinal says, "It may seem like a lot to get used to."

"No, not really," I tell her, trying to keep my tone light. I'm annoyed at myself. I turned nineteen in February; I'm no child to be upset that Big Rock Candy Mountain turns out to not be a real place. "I live at a university campus actually. Lived. A big one. This doesn't look so strange."

But it does, somehow. Henryk and I have had more than one conversation about this, about architecture and all its coded messages, and how we know — how we have been provided with irrefutable proof — that there was a before, and that we are living in its aftermath. Because we, back home, live in buildings we could never build now. So the reminder is constant rather than intermittent. That the humanity of the cities failed, that there was a schism between the then and the now. Back Then, before the fall, they could have looked at anything and said: *We know how to reproduce that. We can do that again.* For anything they wished, for anything they saw, whenever they wanted. A skyscraper, a ziggurat, a pyramid, a monument, they had all the knowledge and the resources and the fuel and the labour and the transportation to simply rebuild anything that had come before. We don't. We can't. We cannot even repair the buildings on campus any more. *That's* how we know there was that rift. That's how we know a world ended. By what was lost.

My window looks down onto a few buildings and up to fewer, all graceful arches and catwalks, bridges and roundels, everything carpeted with moss, lichen, and tufty bits of grass just beginning to green up. Thousands of windows gather the day's clouded light. There is no dome. Only mountain and sky.

Dr. Gibson peers down with me, perhaps sensing my confusion or disappointment; or perhaps he just gets this question a lot from new students.

"The *original* facility began as a linked set of domes." He taps the window with his pen, indicating four modest hemispheres barely visible behind the other buildings, clustered like apples half-buried in snow. "The population outgrew those, and they've been repurposed into, if I may say so, a very nice museum and botanical garden. Over time, the original experiment proved successful, and administration decided to protect the facility, as well as the surrounding ecosystem, with a more environmentally unobtrusive method."

"What?"

"Oh, there's a neat little video about it during your orientation sessions," he says dismissively. He returns to my bed and runs his hand across its attached screen of black plastic, generating images, graphs, figures, bright and clear as if they were leaping off the surface. I'm dying of curiosity, but I can't look at the screen and out the window at once, so I go back to the bed too.

"You're pretty anemic," he murmurs, tapping a column of numbers. "Often the case for new students, nothing to worry about. Do you have periods?"

"Usually."

"Don't think we'll need an infusion. I'll just put in a scrip to the kitchen, and it should sort itself with your meals. I'll test again in a few weeks. And it would help with your *Cadastrulamyces* treatment."

For no good reason I'm lying on the bed again, staring up at the ceiling. From the corner of my eye I watch Dr. Gibson's hands move my unfeeling legs back under the blanket, tucking in my hands. "Reid. Reid! Can you hear me? I'm snapping my fingers. Which side?"

"Left. Did I faint?"

"Your leg went," he lies. "This is better; I don't want you to fall on the floor."

My ears are ringing. I try not to imagine how my face looks. Raw, animal desperation, like a starving pet fed on nothing but crumbs and promises its whole life. "You were saying," I hear myself say with truly hilarious nonchalance. Cardinal hovers over his shoulder.

He explains. Not a cure, which is why he said treatment. But a targeted antibody attached to a specially designed synthetic liposome that, for all intents and purposes, puts the symbiont into remission — a deep sleep of exhaustion — because it can no longer use its host's blood glucose for energy. The antibody comes in a flood, and your own immune cells help boost it.

"The disease will still live in you. But it will be metabolically inactive, and your symptoms will be gone, that's the one thing we can promise. It's not a hundred percent effective — I mean, nothing is. It has to be administered on an ongoing basis; for someone your age and weight, probably every four weeks to prevent remission. The side effects of the treatment are minimal. Some soreness around the injection site is common."

I don't care if it has to be injected straight into my eyeball. I don't care if it burns like vinegar. Still I don't speak. I look up at Cardinal's eyes, those gold rings, and I think of sleeping dragons, all claws and teeth on top of their hoard. The first book I remember reading by myself was *The Hobbit* — it must have been a beautiful edition once, corrugated by water at some point but still legible. And with illustrations like stained glass windows. If you feared death, if you loved your life, you would not go near the dragon.

But they do, the whole ragtag gang of them. It's not that they desire the treasure more than they fear death. Only that they think they can cheat it . . .

All those claws. All those teeth. Breath like a lick of flame from the sun. Adventurers. To leave the past behind you on the road, run towards a future gleaming with gold, start anew unencumbered. Say you're a burglar, say you're anything. Pretend you're someone else till you become someone else.

For just a moment, while they wait for me to reply, I think of Henryk's mocking voice in the mountains, asking me who exactly I thought I was.

I don't know. This is my first chance to find out who I am without the adversary. I thought I would have to battle it the whole time I am here, but now they are saying I could be . . . myself. I could be extraordinary to match this brave new world. Not let it out-extraordinary me. I am leaving you behind too, parasite.

"Yes," I tell him. "I want it. Do I have to sign anything? I'll sign it."

The shot is a mere pinprick, barely felt; its only evidence afterwards is a drop of my anemic blood, welling like a tear.

Dr. Gibson hands me a white fabric square. "Press on that for a minute."

I look at the injection site and under my very fingers I watch the weather change. Just below the scratched and translucent surface of my skin, where the fungus lives as near to the open air as it can get while still being inside me, always reminding me it exists, the inky curlicues twist as if caught in a high wind . . . then recede.

There is no sound in the room except my fast shallow breath. Blueblack tendrils fade to the colour of a vein, vanish. The green ones writhe sickeningly fast, like worms; then they too are gone. My heart is hammering. Is it real? Can it be real? Did they bring me here just to fool me with this illusion? I can't even think.

It has always been the rumour that they have a cure here in the domes. Now I know it's true. Cardinal is watching me, enjoying the wonder on my face. But you kept it here, I want to say. You didn't give it to the world once you had it. Why not?

The last viridian tangle whips about like a tail vanishing into a burrow, and then it is gone, everything is gone and I am alone. Really alone, like any normal person.

I peel away the white square marked with a perfect circle of red. I feel lightheaded. They have handed me the hammer and chisel to shape myself into something new and that was all it took: thirty seconds. Nothing has prepared me for this. "All done."

"Marvellous," says Dr. Gibson. "Well, let's get you settled in."

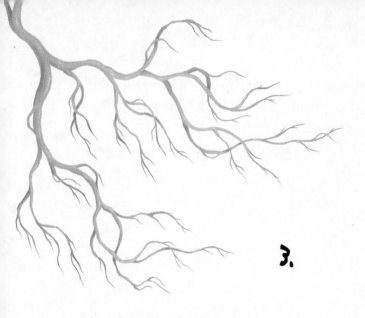

3.

I had worried about how the clothes I brought would be received here, but a seemingly infinite variety of blue-and-white components are on offer in my room's gigantic closet: shirts, pants, coats, jumpsuits, skirts, socks, shoes, boots, gloves, hats, scarves, enough to assemble a thousand outfits. Clearly there's a dress code. Eventually the cast on my ankle casts the deciding vote on what's easiest to wear, and I go exploring.

There are no stairs. All the ascents and descents are grandly curved, and so gradual as to be almost imperceptible. Maps of the campus are displayed at regular intervals, on the ubiquitous light-up wall screens as well as in Braille, relief, and audio recordings. I cannot help but stare every time I pass one. They're so *sharp*, so focused — ironically none of the printed images I've seen of these could represent just how different they are from a printed image. The light they give off is bright enough to illuminate even the tiniest details, but not so bright as to hurt your eyes. No one could have designed this place better for incoming students that might have a physically debilitating disease. One tends to notice these things.

I don't know if I'm awake at an unreasonable hour or if everyone is gathered somewhere else (a burst of paranoia before I recall that there's still a week before orientation and then classes), but I see no one as I make my way to my building's Student Assistance office. My booted foot, sproinging along on its squeaky plastic helper, announces my presence long before I reach the open door. Already a tall boy is standing, smiling, holding out a hand.

"Hi! I'm Jayden, I'm this year's RA. Welcome to Prentice Hall. It's Reid Graham, right? You just got in yesterday? I saw your name pop up on the list this morning. Room fifty-seven. What can I help you with?"

"Um, this is going to sound ridiculous," I begin, letting him lead me to a chair next to his small square desk. "But I was wondering . . . is there any chance I could, uh, share a room with someone?"

He stares at me; I sit and carefully prop my heel on the floor at the recommended angle. It's mostly old guys back home named Jayden (or Brayden or Drayden or Hayden). Funny to see one here; I wonder if he was named after a father or grandfather. He might be a few years older than me, something polished or sanded about him: smooth tan forehead, smooth dark blond hair, lustrous but blank eyes.

"No chance, huh," I prompt him after several seconds. I sensed rather than knew it was a long shot; the building design seems weirdly intent on one to a room. But I've never slept comfortably alone, and last night I couldn't even convince myself that there were other people on my floor, or in the university, or the entire world, and I got so worked up at every little noise and unfamiliar thing in the darkness that I didn't sleep at all. But I don't want to explain to this glittery, patronizing creature that I'm tired of experiencing all-new terrors this week and I want to see if I can mitigate at least one.

"This is really adorable," he finally says, reaching for his tablet. "It really is. It'll be like reuniting a kid and their teddy bear. You know, I just love this job? You get so many interesting stories. I never thought there'd be two of you asking. I'll just sound her room and see if she's up."

The sun is fully up by the time I move my belongings into the new room and ensure the system knows I'm there, which requires Jayden to do some troubleshooting to convince the room monitor to talk to my new watch. This is a procedure so arcane that I only get through it, in my sleep-deprived state, by pretending I am watching a very boring magic spell being cast by some kind of wizard-bureaucrat.

"Did it work?" my new roommate asks from the closet when he's gone. "Wow, it pulled our stuff apart automatically onto two rods. This place is cloud cuckoo land, man."

"I think so," I call back. "I'm Reid, by the way."

"Clementine Dawson, don't call me Clem." She steps out, batting clothes away from her head, a short, thin girl with bushy black hair and a spray of dark freckles across her face from her upper lip to just above her eyebrows, like a burglar's mask. Without meaning to, I clock her for symptoms of Cad and see three missing fingers and most of one ear gone, and her forearms and hands wrinkled with old white scars, though nothing visible remains of the disease itself. She must have taken the treatment too. None of my business. "When did you get here?" she adds.

"Yesterday."

"I've been here a week," she says, sitting on her bed. "Came up from Calgary. I was gonna say I could show you the ropes, but this place has too many ropes. I can't even believe I'm here in the first place, and now I gotta deal with all *this*? It's like taking a degree before taking a degree. What happened to your leg? That on the way here?"

"Uh . . . yeah." I find myself reluctant to say *Bit by a pig*, because it leads into *And someone died*. Maybe I'll tell her later.

"I haven't been able to sleep," she says, lowering her voice. "Glad as hell you showed up. None of the other folks want to share a room. *Don't you want your privacy?* they said. Yeah but I don't know, I guess not as much as they do."

"Yeah, that's how I felt. I just . . . I kept trying to sleep. I had bad dreams. And then every little noise . . ."

"Every. Noise." She gets up and begins to paw through the few items I've placed on the top of my low dresser. "This is better. More like home. Having someone here, I mean. Not the rest of this. Mmm, this soap smells amazing. You get it here?"

"No, that's from home."

I know what she means by *the rest of this*. It's been one day, and my brain feels overstuffed with information, almost nauseated, as if I've been invited to some huge party, a wedding maybe, but instead of five or six dishes there are hundreds, and I not only am expected but forced to get a bite of everything, long past the point I'm full and queasy.

The rest of this includes the lights (touch panel or voice activated rather than the oil lamps or candles back home or, God forbid, a plain switch like the ones that decorate all our walls), the modular furniture that slides across the floor on invisible tracks to transform into desk, bed, chair, sofa, stepstool, storage, the whispery unfamiliar fabrics finer than anything we can weave even from plastic, the constant filtered breeze from the vents, the windows that turn opaque or clear at a touch, even my standard-issue tablet (aside from the silver label with my name on it, a featureless slab of black plastic so thin I'm terrified of breaking it just turning it on), and its accompanying watch, which is like some hyperintelligent but needy little pet on my wrist that I have to check constantly.

I feel like a monkey stumbling around in a museum, unable to parse any of the informational plaques, only able to point at something now and then like, "That's a tree in that painting, I know what a tree is." I had worried that coming here would make me a Morlock slouching into the garden of the Eloi, but I'm something worse — I'm the time traveller, human enough in appearance that they have all inadvertently given me too much credit.

"You eat yet?" Clementine says.

I am grateful that she has disrupted a line of thought that seems to be building into a panic attack. "I had some oatmeal yesterday at the infirmary."

"Yeah, that's what they gave me the first few days. They don't wanna, like, shock our systems," she says knowledgeably, crossing the room to a barely visible panel set into the wall. "So you haven't used the kitchen yet? I can show you that at least. It's weird as hell. Like everything else here."

She waves her watch vaguely at the top of the panel, which immediately springs to life, displaying four blue rectangles whose text I can't read from the bed. "See? Four options programmed for me, because it's my watch. Who programs it? Who knows. How'd they decide what to pick? Beats me. So I press something, who cares, let's say two today." The choices disappear, replaced with a round red clock counting down from five hundred.

She returns to her bed. "Like I said, they're weirdos here but at least they figured out all their food is gonna kill folks like us. Too rich, too salty, too sweet, too everything. There's pills for it, but you gotta make sure you hit the button in the display if you want them. I recommend it myself. Or else you'll, you know. Shit your guts out. The kids from here don't have that problem. It's just us, the uh, whatever. Out of towners."

"Do they have a . . . name for us?" I ask cautiously. "The students coming in from the cities, versus the ones who are already here? Or can people tell?"

She gives me a pitying look. "People can tell."

"I figured."

"Anyway no, not that I've heard. Or not that they'd say around me. Ding! Here we go. Your turn."

I follow her to the panel, from which she retrieves a rounded-edged white plastic box. Lifting the lid reveals a child's storybook idea of breakfast: lurid red tomatoes, golden cubes of potato, two items that resemble fried eggs but which I instinctively feel are merely very good imitations, and two flat items that I am much more comfortable saying are definitely imitations of something, but I don't know what.

"What's the pink stuff?"

"Haven't figured that out yet. It's good though. Salty as all hell."

My single option, boringly, is a bowl of minimally sweetened oatmeal. It arrives with eight slices of apple and a tiny extra compartment containing two pills, which Clementine advises me to swallow first. The kitchen also provides us each tea, in white mugs which I have to admit are fantastically useful and well-designed, right down to the fit of the lids and the grippy texture of their handles. I wonder if I can steal some to take home when I graduate. Mom would love a mug like this. "Where do you want to eat?"

"Okay, that's another thing," she complains, sitting on one of the cubes flanking the cube that comprises the centre of, I guess, our living room. "I have been *looking* for some kinda cafeteria or lunchroom or something. The map doesn't show one. Or if it does, it's called something else. And I asked my watch and I asked this flat bastard here too. I really think they just . . . eat in their rooms. Everybody eats in their rooms. Alone."

"Even the kids?"

"I haven't seen any kids here."

"Weird. Well, I don't want to eat in here all the time. We'll get bugs. I don't care how advanced this place is, bugs are more advanced than people every time."

"That's exactly what I said! See, you and me, we're gonna get along."

My first instinct — which I recognize as a relic from home that does not belong here — is to find another human being and ask. Clementine admits this was hers too, but she resisted it. I don't have to ask her why. She's like me, too accustomed to doing things together and not alone. But now that there are two of us, we prowl the silent, plant-bedecked halls until we find another student who looks easy to corner.

This one doesn't bother with the *polite* part of *politely confused*, as Jayden did — although I suppose as a public-facing administrator he's used to putting on faces. "A what?"

"All right, maybe you don't call it a cafeteria," I clarify. "But like, a lunchroom or dining hall or . . . ?"

"Uh, no. Not sure why you think we'd have something like that." He moves backwards none too subtly, till his coat rustles against the dangling ivy of the wall behind him and there is nowhere left to go. "Do you, uh, know how to use the kitchen panel in your room? Did someone show you? You can get food right in your room. There's a Student Assistance office in —"

"Oh, forget it." I push down my anger at his condescension, then freeze, listening for the internal voice — but there is nothing. Anger, which I am used to, which is ordinary, and yet no response inside me except me. No subtle nudges from the adversary urging me to flee instead, no stiffening of my wrists or knees as if I'm about to start a fight and it would rather I didn't. No Cad. It really is gone. Not that I didn't believe it, just . . .

Clementine is tugging on my sleeve, asking if I'm okay, if it's my leg, do I need help, and the boy takes the opportunity to eel away from us and escape.

"Fucken snob," Clementine mutters. "Forget it. We'll just go back to the room."

"I . . . yeah. That's fine." I feel not quite broken but dislocated: everything intact, just in the wrong place. As if a part of me had turned away from another part of me and then turned again to look back at it. If the theories are right, I've had Cad all my life, even though I was officially diagnosed at fourteen. Always it has been in me, demon, guardian, malevolent spirit, watchdog. Pouring its poison into my veins. But now it's just me and I am a stranger to myself.

"Yeah. I think I should lie down."

On the way back, I'm drawn by a hot shaft of light falling across the floor that wasn't there half an hour ago; the morning's fog must have cleared. We follow it to what's obviously intended to be a study space — barely distinguishable from similar spaces back home, except that everything here is ferociously rectilinear plastic in shades of green, blue, and grey instead of wood or metal. One whole wall is window, all unfrosted.

"Jackpot!" Clementine claims a table and cracks open her breakfast. "Ugh, everything is cold. They should insulate these things like they do with the mugs."

"Why bother if everyone eats in their rooms?"

"I guess." She shudders theatrically. "Wanting to be alone all the time is some serial killer shit," she proclaims. "It's not mentally healthy."

"They'd probably say the same thing about *not* wanting to be alone. It's just . . . part of the culture we'll have to get used to."

I stir my oatmeal while she describes all the ways she plans to refuse assimilation into this batshit ear-collecting murderparty standoffish campus so-called culture; the torrent of words is kind of soothing. Most of my friends back home are no great talkers. Nadiya was always joking and riffing off something, but someone else had to get her going, and Henryk loves nothing better than a long silence in the middle of a conversation.

Forget it. They're not here. They belong to that space I will have to wall off inside myself for at least four years. I can be a new person here, after all. No one knows me. I don't even know myself. Do I.

"Excuse me? Uh, is it . . . do you mind if . . . is it all right if I . . . ?"

"Come on in," I say without turning around; Clementine would warn me if it was an actual serial killer, I feel. "Place doesn't belong to us."

The newcomer is quite a young-looking girl, but surely they don't admit twelve- or thirteen-year-olds. She's even shorter than Clementine, something feline in her smallness and quickness. And she has something of us, too, about her, which I try to pin down as Clementine effortlessly pulls her into conversation and I eat my bland, claggy breakfast. Something unsettled in the clothes, I think — as if she, like me, has grown up wearing either hand-me-downs or sensibly oversized you'll-grow-into-them clothes and the novelty of the form-fitting uniform pieces has not worn off yet.

And then the accent — to my ears she doesn't have one, nor does Clementine. But Dr. Gibson, Dr. Cardinal, Jayden, and the boy we accosted this morning do. It's the first accent I've ever encountered in my life — heard in person, that is, not just read an approximation of in a book. And it's subtle, only found in the *o*'s and the *u*'s, something wide and round that seems to make some words take up more space in a sentence than they should. I suppose that makes sense. If you've been segregated in one place for seventy or eighty years it's quite reasonable to sound different from the place you've left.

More students straggle in, apparently grateful to have found a gathering place, all newcomers accepted to Howse for the upcoming semester, and then, presumably out of curiosity at the noise of our chattering rather than a desire to participate in it, someone local. At first, because the sun washes out his shape, he is only a slender line of blue and white, and then he sits next to me, out of the direct rays. Very tall and thin, short hair, skin the kind of brown that verges on midnight-blue. His large, long-lashed eyes are also brown, ringed with a thin perimeter of dark blue, as if chosen to match. For one dazzled second I wonder if that's something you can actually do here, change your eye colour to suit your tastes, I'd believe anything about this place at this point, any technological accomplishment, but I clamp my lips shut before I can ask.

"Is this seat taken?" he asks.

"Nobody's sitting in it."

He carries no food, only a mug of something that doesn't smell like our tea — something rich and complex. I try to sneak a glance at it, but the liquid level is too low.

"I'm St. Martin," he says. "I'm from Howse. First-year environmental science."

I appreciate that he's given me a structure to introduce myself with in turn. Is that his first name or his last name? "Reid. From Edmonton. Ditto."

He smiles, showing beautifully even teeth. "Congrats on getting accepted into the program."

There's that accent: *Coungrats. Prugram.* I feel oddly pleased to have pinned it down. "Hey, so you've seen a bunch of . . . of new people come in every year, right? If you're from here?"

"That's right."

"Do you guys have a name you call us and something else you call yourselves? It's not important. It's just my roommate and I were wondering."

St. Martin laughs, covering his mouth with his hand. "Not that I've ever heard," he finally manages. "But if we made one up, I think it should be something about coffee. You folks just have no filter."

"Yeah?"

"Yeah. You say whatever you want."

"And you don't?"

"Emphatically no. We do not." He sips his drink, still chuckling. "You'll get used to it. Everybody does."

The others are talking more excitedly now, bringing the room to a level of noise I'm more used to — the noise of the Dining Hall, back home. The hum of humanity. We are all from outside, except for St. Martin and, I think, three others. The locals have Jayden's kind of poreless, groomed look to them — everyone is a pot recently glazed and fired. None of the locals show any visible signs of Cad. I tell myself to stop it, stop staring, stop being a yokel, a rube.

Everyone says where they came from and I tell myself not to notice that the same city never comes up twice. Everyone says what they are studying. The very young girl tucks her short red hair behind her ear and says she's taking English literature and I did not even know you could do that. I realize that her tiny face is marked, like mine, with dozens of scrapes and cuts, all fresh and angry. They really put you through the wringer to get here. I wonder how many kids get the acceptance letter and never make it to the gates.

One by one, the breakfast boxes are scraped clean. How do they make their food here? It's not flat enough to farm,

I didn't spot terracing, and you sure can't raise any livestock bigger than a goat, unless they've trained cows to climb mountains. Is it machines, robots? Do they use bacteria, like for the paper of my acceptance letter? I suppose I don't need to know right away; I've got four years, at least, to find out.

The important thing, I think, is that my oatmeal tastes like oatmeal. A little bit of honey was provided in a sealed white plastic packet, and the honey tastes like honey. Did it come from bees? Is beekeeping the sign of a highly advanced place or a primitive one? Which one are they? Which one were we? What would the bees say? We don't even always *have* bees on campus back home, although we always have boxes in case some want to move in. You can't force bees to do anything they don't want to do. Which still doesn't tell me whether this is real honey or not.

Clementine is reminiscing, loudly, about the food they eat in Calgary; because they have so much less water, what she's talking about sounds like the food in our bad years in Edmonton. We don't have water sometimes; they don't have it most of the time. We both live, I think, in the very corners of our human habitats, like mice confining themselves to the corner of the cage where there is solid floor instead of a wire grid. But it's still living.

She trails off and elbows me. "What about you, Reid?"

"What about what?"

"We were just saying if there was kind of a festival food. Something special. You know?"

"Oh. Well, it depends on the part of campus, because each hall feeds five or ten buildings and it depends on who's running them. At ours it was . . . um." I'm suddenly very aware of the eyes on me and which belong to whom and that the four Howse students are all smiling encouragingly and that I don't know that I like the smiles even if they are trying to be nice. "Um, it's just pea soup."

There is a pause. Then the red-haired girl sighs, "I *love* pea soup."

And that makes it easier for me to ignore the kindly chuckles of the locals and describe this particular soup: How you can only make it in the spring because it uses fresh peas instead of dried; how it's served by putting a scoop of cooked barley in the bowl first and then gently pouring the frothing green mass overtop (ideally you can still see a little hump sticking out of the surface, like a grassy hill); and then a sprinkle of fried mushrooms, not dried and reconstituted. Then you dig through the greenness and get some soup and the chewy barley and one mushroom on the spoon. How it makes me think of . . . rain in spring. The sweet, safe smell of rain. Safe because if there's any rain at all, we might have another chance for a good year, a quiet year with no disasters. Relief, calm. All that in the first mouthful. A meal you might get just once every few years, because if there aren't enough peas for everyone, then the peas are used for other things. The others are nodding.

"Why not just make less?" one of the Howse students asks, puzzled. Like St. Martin, she did not bring her breakfast box, only the white mug with its fascinating smell. "Let a few people have some soup, instead of nobody at all. You could do a draw for it maybe? So it's fair?"

"Everybody gets some or nobody gets some," I say, equally puzzled. We stare at each other for a while. Her eyes are very green. This is something we don't even need to teach the five-year-olds back home, so I know she's making fun of me, but no one's laughing. I feel a small, piercing surge of anger, like a wasp sting.

Jayden breaks the awkward silence by rushing in, waving his tablet. "St. Martin! I have a question about . . . oh, is it a party?"

"We're just eating breakfast," Clementine says.

He laughs. "Aw! Pretty good stuff compared to back home, huh?" he says. "I bet you were dreaming about the food here the whole way!"

"No," says Clementine, and I shake my head. In fact, I hadn't been thinking of it at all, even when I was hungry in the mountains. I hadn't realized it till he said it.

"I mean it's not like we were going hungry, at least not where I'm from," I say, feeling slightly defensive. "It's not like here, sure. But there's a hell of a lot more edible plants than not. You can eat like ninety percent of the landscape if you know what you're doing."

"It's amazing," Jayden says brightly, shaking his head. "Amazing. Every year I listen to you people, and every year I'm just delighted. It's like animals learned to talk. Isn't it? Like a dog just learned how to talk, and it's talking to another dog that doesn't know the trick. 'Oh, you can just eat everything you find!'"

A few people chuckle; I realize my mouth is hanging open. For a moment St. Martin looks as if he will say something in reply, *That isn't what she meant and you know it*, but I speak first.

"So I bet you spend a lot of time volunteering to help the people outside the domes find food, right? Since you seem to like the idea of feeding stray dogs."

Jayden blinks. "Well, we —"

"Don't give your food away. Sure. I get it. We're not really worth leaving home for."

This time he remains silent. My face burns, anticipating the protests of the other Howse students — at a minimum I expect them to tell me to shut up. But they all look away.

"We don't really have anything *organized* for that kind of thing," St. Martin says quietly.

I almost ask him why not, but they've already told me. Instead I say, "Well, maybe *I'll* start something."

"Start . . . what, exactly?"

I bare my teeth at Jayden, not quite a smile. "Helping the people who dream about your food."

The room empties out after that. Clementine and I remain, bathing in the sunlight even though it has weakened again with the fog. I go to the window with my mug, still rattled. Stone, stone, stone, lichen, moss. The landscape is like a painting done with a palette knife. How Yash and Mal would love this. No, I can't think about them, or I'll die of homesickness. I'm still blushing; my face feels hot, my ears.

"What a dickdrop," Clementine says dismissively. "You don't have to talk to those."

"I know." I'm still staring at the planes of the view: diagonals, uprights. How does anybody study anything here? I could look at this all day. I am from a place where the landscape was built by human hands. Here no matter where you look another detail is waiting to be noticed: a perfectly round stone, a tiny pine tree, a patch of flowers (pale pink, grey leaves), a hopping crow. They have kept their trees here, I mean living trees, old trees. Not like back home where even the largest and oldest trees eventually gave up after years of drought. "We're gonna keep eating here, right?"

"Hell yeah. It isn't even a matter of if I want to any more," Clementine says. "First off because eating in our rooms is bullshit. We're not in jail. And secondly because everybody else new wants to eat with other people. And if we keep it up, they'll feel better about coming. Right?"

"Right. Because they kinda don't seem to give a shit about that here." I lean heavily on the windowsill. "It's funny. They do have a name for us. It's *you people*."

The other thing that's funny, which I resolve to keep at the back of my mind, is how easily, even effortlessly, they explained why the university never opened its doors to save the dying world. They're just not good at sharing.

"This thing you said you were going to start," Clementine says, and I wait for her to finish the sentence, but she's clearly waiting for me to do the same.

I shrug. "I didn't really think it through. I just wanted them to say out loud that they know damn well how hungry people are — that it's *not* a case of not knowing. But now that I'm saying it, yeah. Can they stop us? From starting a . . . a student club, or a group, or something? To organize aid outside the domes?"

"Guess you'll find out."

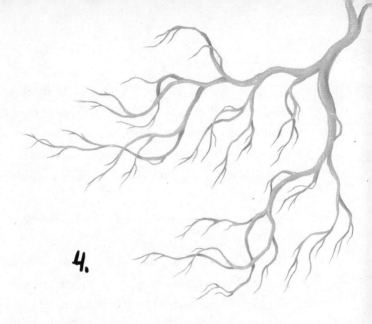

4.

Class is better. Surrounded by bodies, being fed knowledge, like back home. This defensive wall of humanity I carry in my head is now real, visible, and I feel calmer. So far Clementine and I have managed not to get sick of one another's company — helped along, of course, by the fact that she has befriended at least a dozen other people in the week since orientation. But it makes me feel less homesick, having someone always at my side.

That it is not Henryk still grates, often and painfully. The *novelty* grates. I had always taken for granted how much of my life already had every rough edge rubbed off it from constant use, everything from the stairs in my building to my childhood friends. Every awkward moment, deep secret, squirming insecurity was dragged out of us long ago and brought into the light to be interrogated. Now I must navigate this again and I find I don't much like it. Clementine makes it look easy; people love her at once, as I did. Warily, I occasionally talk to St. Martin, who perhaps as expiation for that first day — even though he was much less annoying than Jayden — has volunteered as unofficial ambassador and translator while we're getting settled in. But I wouldn't call him a friend.

"All right, everyone, you can look in Exercises for what we're doing today."

This too I'm still getting used to. Next to me Clementine mutters and swears, swears and mutters. The touchscreen doesn't like her fingers. I swipe through my tablet clumsily, reminding myself that it is like a building with rooms and doors. Main Page is the entrance room. Then you find the door you need (Live Materials) and you go into the room; then you find the next door (Soil 1 — Tuesday/Thursday) and you go into its room and you pick up the book marked Exercises.

Text blooms across the screen and I am still not tired of that, I still love it, it is like watching an irrigation pipe flood a field, turning the deadened soil from pale to dark. Black, the colour of hope, life. I tell no one. They mock you for remarking upon any amazing thing here. You are supposed to take it all in whole, like swallowing a stone.

Our instructor Karina (they don't like the word *professor*, which I find inexplicably funny) is a fat pleasant woman with expressive hands, which she flicks around her head as if she's signing, which she is not. The two tiny cameras near the front of the room whizz patiently back and forth on their tracks, sending video to students who didn't feel like leaving their rooms today. They have their work cut out for them, those cameras; Karina is in constant motion.

"Environmental monitoring!" she says, and the words appear on the white screen behind her. "Let's talk about options by media: soil, surface water, groundwater, and air. Am I missing anything?"

Pens scribble over tablets and words begin to coalesce on the screen behind her; she doesn't turn, watches us, smiles. Mine is moving as furiously as everyone else's. I've been thinking about this.

Wildlife

Fauna   Wildlife movement, reproduction, predation, health

Fauna

Vegetation   Vegetation health

Vegetation health, nutrient content, species richness

Biodiversity

Species richness   Habitat potential, nesting sites, denning sites, leks, nursery streams, etc.

Solar radiation   Wind

Precipitation   Pptn

Pptn

I put my hand up when my answer doesn't appear on the board. This keeps happening. I hear a rushing sound in my ears and I file it away for later, because that too keeps happening. It's a small class. Forty pairs of eyes are on me. I look up at my hand: Still no markings. Still a miracle. I wish I could stop looking at my hands to confirm that I am who I think I am though. I think people are noticing.

"Yes, Reid?"

"My connection seems to be down again," I say apologetically. "What about remote sensing? Lidar, GPR, infrared? Drones or satellites? For things like vegetation cover and surface water and some of the other parameters we're talking about."

Her smile freezes, though as always I sense no hostility in her. This isn't in our textbook; I checked. It's also minimally described in the other literature that St. Martin showed me and Clementine how to look up in the library. Most of what I know about it I know from the books back home. There's one for you: we knew something they don't. Except I don't think that's it. I don't think so at all.

I'm pretty sure they have their own satellites here. I don't know how I'd confirm it. But if they're up there, they were sent up to monitor the landscape — the domes in particular — and that's how their tracker necklaces work. She knows exactly what I'm talking about.

"We won't be discussing that," Karina says pleasantly. "It's not relevant to the class. Now, this is a good list, everyone! We'll dig into each of these and how they interact with one another as the semester goes on. Chemically, hydrologically, thermally, biologically. Let's start with soil, since it's the main media affecting parameters in surface water and groundwater."

I mechanically take notes and watch her flying hands. Eventually the noise in my ears dies down. All the windows are open and I watch dust motes, insects, the occasional seed-puff float inside the classroom. Pollen crowns bowed heads. Birds are calling to one another outside, parents asking if the kids need anything when they go out.

My hand moves. My mind stays still. I think about *Watership Down*, the shockingly pristine paperback Henryk and I found in a collapsed apartment after an earthquake. I think about the warren where you could not ask anyone where another rabbit was. They wouldn't answer you. Just change the subject. And when rabbits disappeared they were never mentioned again even in memoriam.

I think about the questions they didn't answer during orientation. How I put up my hand and asked and received no answer. I think about the way people avoid my gaze when I ask them if they're interested in signing up for my fledgling aid group, Share the Bounty. Is it the name?

Here, you can ask anything except *What did you do in the past?* They live in the now so furiously that they almost seem afraid to look back. And I cannot understand this. How can you do anything without using the past as its foundation? I tell the story of myself in present tense, but they use future. And they think of themselves as assets that will appreciate or depreciate, also in the future, instead of a system in motion, with a then and a now and a later. They are a warren filled with rabbits that are physiologically incapable of reversing direction in a tunnel even when there's room.

"Hands-on exercise!" Karina trills. The board behind her flashes white, all the words gone as if they never existed.

We file outside into the cool spring air, wet and resinous, and as always I stop to stare up at the view: the sky, the grey and lavender peaks, the dark trees, stubborn specks of snow at the summits. A huge alpine bumblebee roars into my elbow, ricochets off in a puff of pollen, and heads off at a more sedate pace.

Labs are held in the building next door, long and low and practically built out of windows, or so it seems.

"It can be hard to tell which type of glass is which around here," Karina says as we head towards the entrance. "These ones up here are transparent solar panels, which most of the roof and some of the upper windows are made of — if you look closely, you can see they're slightly bluer than the ones below them. They also have thicker frames, to hold the mechanism that tilts them fractionally during the day for efficiency. You'll have noticed everything on campus is electric; nearly all of it comes from these panels."

"Do you have geothermal?" I ask before I can stop myself.

This time she doesn't seem to mind. "Well caught, Reid! You're thinking, If there's *anywhere* we might have it, it'll be in the *mountains*. We'll be talking about that in a few days, the geological setup here and how it compares to the rest of the country. Quite right. We do have a geothermal system."

"For heat exchange, or for electricity generation?"

"Heat. Unfortunately, it doesn't go quite deep enough to reach a thermal stratum useful for generation. There are really only a few areas in the province where it would be possible."

"And when was it drilled?"

She pivots. "In we go! Room five. Everybody pick a bench and make sure you've got five soil samples. We'll talk about where they came from after the exercise."

You can't ask where anybody is in that warren. You will receive no knowledge for your trouble. And you can submit to the secrecy and suffer for your ignorance, or investigate and be punished for it. One or the other. One or the other. Bigwig almost dies because you cannot ask *where*.

Every day I test them like this. Every day the answer is the same. No one here wants you to learn any history. Why? To fix your gaze on the future is . . . well, laudable, if limited. To look at the present is inevitable. But the constant gentle relentless redirection means that we can no longer look at where we came from, us outsiders. Because we came *from* the past. We have all come from places where time stood still for a little while, then began to move backwards. And for them in here, it moved forward. Why not let us say it? Why not acknowledge it? What would I have to do to make them see us as people?

I put my head down and follow the instructions on the tablet, half paying attention. The exercise is about soil texture, doing a hand texture versus hydrometer, and it's supposed to take most of the afternoon, though I can't imagine why.

"Oh, very good, Reid!" Karina pauses at my bench, setting down her tablet to examine mine. "You're done all five?"

"I've done this before."

"Your *numbers* are very good."

"They better be, for all the time I spent doing this back home," I say, since it seems to have not sunk in the first time. "Honestly, I've taught kids to do this around twelve or thirteen. Because it's interesting and it's useful and we all have to know as much about soil as possible." To survive, I almost add, but I don't want to state the obvious.

"Oh! You used to teach science out there?"

I shrug. Something about *out there* rubs me the wrong way even though, looked at from every angle, it's perfectly accurate. Fewer kids every year makes it easier, anyway, to do the few exercises we can still do. Nobody says anything about it but everyone notices it.

She marks my grade at the top of the exercise sheet and closes the file, then she moves on to the other benches, humming, unperturbed.

I think of what Aldous Wong, our erstwhile track star, everybody's crush, victim of a galloping mountain of meat, told me just before our disastrous hunt. *Bait. Wait. Aggravate.* They won't take my bait. Now what?

Clementine doesn't want to go to the museum with me, so I head over alone, limping carefully along the smooth, spotless paths. While on the one hand the lack of stairs makes me nervous — a stairwell is a good place to hide in case of fires or storms if you cannot get out or get underground — I appreciate it. Back home is crammed with stairs. All the elevators sulk in basements, unwanted and unable to be repurposed. But it's like they don't expect disasters here.

A tap with my watch secures my admission and downloads a map to my tablet, but I stuff the tablet into my backpack and walk the empty halls unguided, both hands free, as if I've gone on a scavenging trip through the city. More homesickness. Henryk and Nadiya and I prowling through the streets, pretending we were looking for hidden treasure, going to the neighbourhoods everyone told us not to go to, digging through the rubble of ruined houses looking for wood or glass or books or toys, giggling at our pirate names. What had mine been again? Three landlocked children with pocketknives for cutlasses.

In front of each exhibit, stepping onto the hexagonal pad causes a screen to light up and a soft voice to start. I stand carefully for each one, swallowing anxiety like saliva. They showed us videos during orientation — two days of incredibly cheerful volunteers in matching T-shirts (bright yellow, to stand out from the sea of blue and white), showing us our classrooms, sending us on scavenger hunts around campus, breaking us into teams to get "points," and trying to impress upon us the need for secrecy — basically apologizing, in a lightly unserious fashion, for sedating and kidnapping Us People before we reached the zone marker. I knew which of the students had come from outside and which from in by who laughed at that video.

I knew about videos, I mean to say. I knew about movies. But nothing, nothing prepares you for those first moments of seeing a picture move . . . my whole body broke out instantly in sweat. Clementine and I grabbed simultaneously for each other's hands with such speed that we cracked our knuckles together, not even looking at one another. You do prepare to some degree for the things you read about. It wasn't like we were . . . I don't know. Wild cats. Being confronted with a mirror. But still.

The first few exhibits in the museum are all my kind of thing — the geology of the area, local species, fossils found here. If I can find a fossil here I don't even care if I get my degree or not. I particularly want one of those big ammonites, like they have in the front entryway of Prentice Hall, all hot greens and reds like the northern lights.

There's a hologram of a whiskeyjack, my companion on the long trudge here. Caught one trying to steal my bike bell one morning. It looks so real I almost reach out to stroke the feathery grey head. Funny that they seem so much tamer than the magpies here, whereas back home the campus magpies are so tame they clearly consider themselves people.

Site selection . . . is this what I'm looking for? It's oddly circumstantial, as if it's dancing around a hole in the ground. That long-ago corporation chose this place for their sustainable energy experiment because of its isolation and access to the natural resources discussed in the previous exhibits. But due to internal conflicts, construction didn't begin until it was almost too late to construct it at all — worldwide supply chains were beginning to fail already, from the making of a thing to getting it out of the factory. Fortunately since it was early days, what was needed could still be done with enough money. So they clenched their teeth and paid up, and the four little domes rose bravely from the stone plateau.

They drilled for the geothermal system that warms the buildings in winter and cools them in summer . . . what year? It doesn't say. I frown, and go on. They drilled into the abundant aquifer beneath the site, previously undetected. Since the water was naturally saline, modifications to the water treatment plant were instituted. There's a little model of the water treatment plant, a building I've walked by dozens of times now without knowing what it was — all vertical flutes and curves, like a pipe organ carved out of stone. Initially reverse osmosis used, then, as the research labs got going, less energy-intensive nanofilters.

I watch the model for a long time, till the voice eventually gets tired of repeating itself and dies out. Blue water is from the aquifer, colourless after it runs through the process. There's so much water here. It does something to the mind. For a couple of nights Clementine and I continued to wash ourselves with rags and bowls, swearing each other to secrecy. We just could not fathom a shower. Wasting that much water.

She wondered what the others would say — the insiders, the kids born here — at our casual nudity. "Who cares?" she announced. "It's not like nobody knows what a body looks like. But you know what? I bet they'd clench their assholes about it. I bet I'd get written up if I walked down the hallway in my socks like back home."

"I bet you would."

But I steeled myself to shower one day, when Clementine was out somewhere, and . . . I don't know. I never remember a year when there was enough water to immerse yourself in anything, though Yash and Mal assured me there had been in their youth. The river was dozens of feet deep, they said. Fish and everything. But then every year a little less, a little less, and some years nothing, and everyone panicked, and then it would come back the next year . . . It was like everything else, Yash said. A stuttering stop of everything they had taken for granted. At first more good years than bad, then equal amounts of bad and good, then bad overtaking, and finally no more good. I had never been fully underwater unless you counted the infrequent spring downpour.

That day, I stood under the hot water, shaking, feeling terror rise, fighting it down, trying to pin it in place like a worm: What was I so afraid of? Was it the Cad returning? What was it warning me against? Finally, after what felt like forever, I burst into tears and stepped out, and I knew. My fear was that I was somehow using the *last of the water*, the last of the *good* water, and now everybody would die. Because I was selfish, because I had wasted it. Someone must have said something similar to me or around me when I was a kid, and I had taken it in and tattooed it onto my neurons.

The clock on the wall said I had been in there for seven minutes. It felt like an eternity.

They have so much here. They have everything they could ever want. They even have things they didn't have when they built the domes. They developed the bacterial vats to grow things, fine-tuning them to get the combinations of proteins, fats, lipids, and other matrices they wanted — anything from paper to concrete, from chicken to soap. They stopped enclosing the site within actual domes (originally meant partly as showmanship to the investors, and partly as a genuine effort to prove that the site was self-sufficient and receiving nothing from outside except water and sunshine once it got going).

The engineered nanoceramic panels have been replaced by a much larger and less intrusive system that still serves to keep residents safe from . . . I squint at the little diorama. Wildlife, geological events such as landslides or mudslides, falling stones, falling trees . . . and us, I think. The have-nots. Because this place wasn't built as an experiment for a research facility really, was it? It wasn't about proving concepts of renewable energy and a circular economy. It was built as a prototype to prove to the rich that this was a bunker that could work. If you were careful enough, if you were rich enough, you could buy something just like this and sit in it to comfortably watch the world around you stutter to a stop as it ran out of everything you had bought up just before the end. And it wasn't the end of everything. Only the end of the things they coveted: money, power, comfort.

What does the end mean, anyway, when it's not death? We don't teach the kids back home about Back Then and call it *a collapse*. We don't even refer to the collapse of the Roman empire or the British empire. We tell them no, it doesn't mean everybody died or the physical artifacts and infrastructure of the civilization disappeared or . . . or exploded or whatever. Sometimes it means the governance collapsed. Sometimes irreversible negative changes to things you could measure, like GDP or quality of life or income or poverty or measures of democracy or whatever. Here, now, it also means ecosystem collapse on top of everything else.

The end of the world, no. The end of a world, the one they loved, that's what they couldn't tolerate. That's what they built these to escape.

It's a cynical thought. Nothing in the museum agrees with me. But I feel that I'm right, I feel it in my bones. There's a photograph of the principal scientists: eighteen people and their families. And there's another one, much larger, of the investors. As time went on they must have bought their way in here. A good life, away from the upheaval of the outside world.

It's strange, and yet not so strange (I could have predicted it) that the museum has absolutely no mention of what was going on in the world outside while the domes were being planned, built, and occupied. None.

And in here, they cured Cad. And eventually someone said: *Let's start inviting other people in. From the outside.*

Why?

Only the first dome is the museum proper; I head through a kind of airlock into the first of the other three, converted, as Dr. Gibson said, into a botanical garden. We still have a few greenhouses on campus, so I'm ready for this one. Greenhouses are finicky things. One broken pane overnight and you can lose everything. And we, unlike these people, live in a world of broken things that cannot be repaired. Across the river from us you could still see the points of the Muttart pyramids, the panes broken so long ago that everything inside is dust except for the concrete outlines of the beds that once held rare plants.

The atmosphere is heavy and sweet, and the oxygen hits my desiccated lungs like dunking my head underwater, so that I stand for several minutes simply gasping for air and leaning on the slick wall. Everything is dark and green, everything is tangled and touching, flowers smoulder in red and pink along the curved walls. I can't understand why I'm alone in here. I can't understand why there aren't people *living* in here. *I* would live in here if I could get away with it. I've never seen anything so beautiful and that includes my first glimpse of the mountains.

Their planting scheme mostly follows the old outlines of the buildings, and in a few places they have kept part of the foundations to protect roots or low shrubs, or repurposed small outbuildings to house orchids or bromeliads. Mist floats down from hidden sprayers, the hissing the only sound except for my footsteps on the stone path.

There are too many wonders to take in at once; I'll come back. The next dome is desert, and the final dome is cool and much less densely planted — this one I take to be temperate rainforest, containing mostly coastal plants and trees, including, almost unbelievably, a redwood in the centre. It is a wonder, though its topmost tip is nowhere near the ceiling. I wonder what it will look like in a century or two — whether they will have to open the top to let it grow.

Here too they display remnants of older infrastructure — the drilling rig used for the geothermal setup, an old gas chromatograph, computers, everything protected in its own transparent plastic box studded with moisture and temperature sensors.

Surprisingly, Dr. Cardinal is standing in front of one of the cells, by far the smallest, imprisoning nothing more than a black-covered spiral-bound notebook on a clear plinth, open to two pages of spiky blue Cyrillic handwriting. Even from behind I recognize her: the stance, the swept-back white hair.

Am I allowed to talk to her? Should I? I look at the notebook for a while next to her. There's no information plaque and no voices in here. Silence except for the occasional drip of water.

"Reid," she murmurs. "Settling in? Feeling better, I hope?"

"Much better. I . . . what's this?"

While she explains that it's the very notebook in which Dr. Alexandra Yaremchuk elucidated the metabolic pathway that allowed the first development of a treatment for *Cadastrulamyces*, I try to nod or indicate I'm listening. I am; I just can't move.

None of the numbers on the page seem to show a date. On the top of the right-hand page, a white sticker has been placed in the corner, perhaps obscuring it.

In this warren we don't ask *when*. Because the answer might be, *A cure was found in time to change the entire trajectory of history and prevent the destruction of the systems that made a cure possible.* They didn't share it then and they're not sharing it now. But it was found. Right here. Right in this very facility. Like the flash of brilliance just before the moon entirely obscures the sun during an eclipse.

"And classes are going well?" she goes on, as if I'm not visibly collapsing inside, right beside her.

No, not like that flash of brilliance exactly. More like a cat clinging desperately to something overlooking a precipice, uncaring of what it clawed in order to get purchase for all four limbs. *Purchase*, there's a good one. It means two things.

"They're fine," I tell her mechanically. I could have been born *without* Cad, is that what this means? That my mother would not suffer this disease, that my best friend, Nadiya, didn't have to die without us even being able to say goodbye, that Clementine did not need to suffer as she has, that millions . . . tens of millions . . . of people, animals . . . that they knew *the whole time* and kept it in here. No different from the casual, face-averted cruelty of not giving people food. "Aside from the technology, they're not so different from home, really. A lot of math, memorization, and field-work when we can manage it. Lab exercises. Hands-on things. We don't have textbooks like here. There's a printing press, but we have to be pretty careful with paper."

She's still watching me, leaving a gap in the conversation. Henryk would have just let it sit, I think. Instead I look at the notebook, the fast excited writing, the white pages, the almost microscopic grey dots on it. When you have electricity you don't have to do everything on paper if you don't want. But she liked something about it, this Dr. Yaremchuk.

For a second I wonder whether Cardinal knows everything about the world outside Howse just as she claims to know everything inside. Surely she must. She knows where students are coming from when she sends out those acceptance letters. I don't need to tell her about the years of drought that killed almost all the trees for hundreds of kilometres in every direction, the years without rain, the winters so cold you could do nothing but burn everything around you for warmth. What seemed like an infinite number of trees diminished with horrifying speed after they died. You needed only multiply how much wood to stay warm for one winter by how many decades the trees were being cut down by how many families had to do it . . . and books, after all, are only another kind of tree. We cannot afford to cut down the just-recovering saplings to turn into paper. Better to use chalkboards. Chalk, at least, we've got.

"Did," I begin, my mouth dry, both because I'm afraid she'll answer me and because I know I'm holding the puzzle piece she wants me to fit into the conversation and I'm not putting it in there.

"Yes?"

"Did she . . . did you . . . they . . . did anyone ever find out where Cad . . . came from?"

She watches me for a long time but she will not see Cad on my skin any more; she will not see the trees writhing under my eyelids and fingernails, she will not see them wriggling under my cheeks like Birnam Wood coming to Dunsinane.

Finally she says, "I'm sorry, Reid. We never did. I can tell you've been wondering this for a while."

"Who hasn't?" I hear the bitterness in my voice, but she doesn't recoil from it. She's heard this before. Suddenly I am so weary of the entire conversation I just want to stagger back to my room and lie down. Maybe not get up again. "It doesn't matter anyway. Does it. It's too late."

"Too late for what?"

I wave an arm uselessly — I don't mean the museum, I don't mean Howse University, I mean the world outside it, the world that shivered and broke apart and was too sick to put itself back together. The whole world. Truly it did not matter where it came from once it had gotten itself established. Like so many other things. I thought I wanted answers about it but what difference would it make now?

She says, "I can tell you that we may have been wrong about the name, about how it was initially studied. It's not truly a fungus at all, nor a parasite. Parasitoid would be more accurate. The team believed that it was . . . well, something else, and it was mischaracterized because we wanted to put it into a box of pre-existing characterization and study it using pre-existing techniques. When it began to inhabit humans, it was likely very much its own life form, having absolutely no idea of what to do inside us. Trying to optimize its own survival, and not aware that it's doing so at the expense of a host, because it's unaware it's in a host."

I had guessed that, and I don't know how I guessed. Maybe it told me itself, the adversary . . . maybe it tried to explain to me that a living thing was not where it wanted to live, that it had another home somewhere, that even when it killed it did not know it was killing or wish to kill. That does not make you innocent, I tell the sleeper. It makes you something else. I don't know the word.

I think again: semi-sentient.

At my checkup a few days ago I told Dr. Gibson about how my Cad had punished me once, with that awful, full-body paralyzing agony for using the word *parasite* to describe it, and he listened very carefully while I spoke, as if memorizing every word, then calmly told me no no, it was an unfortunate coincidence of timing, that I happened to have a pain event at just that moment. It wasn't listening to you, he said. It just seemed like it was because of what happened just then. I told him about that last time I felt like I communicated with it, how I thought it helped me jump to save my mother . . . I waited for him to make fun of me and he didn't. What had he said? *Of course I believe you*, he said. *Everyone experiences it differently. And what are we, in the end, but our neurotransmitters? My own mother* . . .

And he had trailed off, the silence telling me everything I would have asked him anyway. I bet his mother was like me; I bet she spoke to it, the thing, the adversary, with hatred, with acceptance, with exhaustion, pain, frustration, as if it really were a demon living inside her. I bet he watched it in terror and confusion. And I bet it killed her. I wanted to offer my condolences. I said nothing.

It wasn't really listening to you. I want to believe him. God I want to believe him. A living being inside me like that, thinking, remembering, learning, knowing . . .

"Cad didn't ruin everything though," I say before I can stop myself. "It was going to happen anyway. No matter what. Right? I mean the weather, the water . . . my neighbours were there for it, you know. Everything started breaking when they were in their twenties. They remember everything. Even before Cad."

Cardinal doesn't nod, only watches me again. I'm beginning to regret coming into the museum. "And of course there was no way you'd know about the resource wars," she says evenly, as if these are not the two most terrible words you could ever put side by side. "Many, many people died and became disabled from those. And the Parthley Exchange."

"No, I don't know about that."

"It sounds worse than it was," she says, almost offhandedly. "Ten nuclear weapons exchanged over five hours, before cooler heads prevailed."

"*What?* Where? When was this? Do people still have *access* to nukes out there? I read about —"

"Reid, all I'm trying to say is, since you have the disease, it's very tempting to blame everything on it," she says. "It really was more like . . . an amplifier. It simply and very firmly prevented every other problem from being solved. Now, would we have solved those without Cad? No one knows. And it's not worth wasting our time on. It's done and there's no changing what happened."

"It still *is* worth the time, because you have the —" I check myself, realizing that I'm shouting at the university president.

"Reid, tell me something. How many people would you say, back on your campus, have Cad?"

"I don't know. I mean, for *sure*? I guess about . . . maybe one in five people? One in six?"

"But you also know it can have a very long latency period."

"Yeah."

"So it could be higher," she prompts. "There could be people who have it and aren't aware of it. You yourself weren't diagnosed till you were fourteen, were you?"

"How did —"

"It might be double that. Do you think that's reasonable, if there's no way of telling during the latency period? If you're saying one in six, could it be . . . one in three? Could it be one in two? Could it be . . . much higher?"

Yes. It could be. Why not? Why not everybody? Why not everybody in the world? Hell, it had already killed off nearly all the livestock before the droughts took the rest. Cows, horses. Dogs, cats, sheep, goats. Rabbits. Birds. A scant percentage of animals seemed to be immune, certainly less than humans. Why *not* everything and everyone? Except . . . "It moves down. Right? Parent to offspring. So it can't be everybody. If that's what you're saying."

She's silent. No. No, I'm wrong about that. Aren't I. It can be transmitted in other ways and *that's* why she's saying it's the whole world. I think of the dead dog in the river valley, the shocking speed of the fruiting body coming from it, the spores . . . but we've never proved it.

She says, "When someone with Cad dies back home, what do they do with the body?"

"Everybody's burned."

"Nobody buried?"

"No. Never."

I feel both that I'm not telling her something new, and that I am. And I feel intensely, uncomfortably, and abruptly that it's one thing for anthropologists to come in to study what they consider a primitive tribe, and another to tell the tribe that's what you're doing, and another still for the tribe to figure it out because the anthropologist doesn't want to say anything. We burn every body, always, whether we know for sure it had Cad or not. Now that I've told her our custom, what will she do with this information? What have I told her simply by coming here?

The notebook, innocent under its plastic, feels to me like Marie Curie's notebooks — exuding invisible menace into my unprotected flesh. I feel I have been standing in front of it too long. Mumbling some excuse, I retrace my steps to the entrance: through the desert, through the jungle, back to the stone and the thin air. I have more questions than I came in here with.

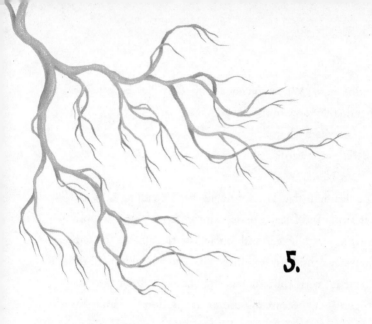

5.

Back home, we teach — not all day, not every day — after harvest and before planting, so the school year spares the growing season, in which every hand is needed to cultivate plants instead of minds. Here, they do it the other way around, letting students dream away the alpine winter. "Do people go home for winter?" I had asked St. Martin when he told me the schedule. He chuckled, and for a moment I readied myself to bristle — he's been a good sport so far about answering questions about this place, which no one else has — but he said, "You want to show off how tough you are, is that it?" and I realized he meant only that getting here had almost killed me, *did* kill others, many others, and that was why only a few dozen outsiders enrolled every year out of the hundreds of acceptance letters sent. Like most of the Howse kids, his own family, he explained, consisted of his parents alone — and they lived on campus, a few blocks from the non-student areas. He could visit whenever he liked. From his tone I guessed that he didn't visit much, but I kept my mouth shut.

"Maintain audiovisual contact!" Karina trills ahead of me, and I automatically glance around at the others, bright in their blue and white amongst the trees. Karina herself flits along the path with deerlike agility despite the pack she carries, far bigger than ours because it is full of emergency equipment and various gadgets for our exercise. She wouldn't let us lighten her load. I am constantly confused by this place. At home my worth is in my labour and effort, and here they are always trying to find ways to refuse it.

I watch my footing, but the trees are spaced widely and the slope isn't too bad here; I can look up and around, taking in the wonder of this place. Living trees! The *smell* of the living trees, the sugary, chemical fragrance of their resin. The needles decaying on the damp ground. Moss, undergrowth. Running water. The glaciers are long gone but they still have snow here, and the lakes never fully emptied out, they say. For every thousand things that perished a few remained. Light bodies skitter amongst the trees, startled at our intrusion: squirrels, birds, butterflies.

"This is amazing," mumbles St. Martin under his breath. "Thank you for —"

"What's amazing to me is that this is everybody's first time doing this," I protest. "I didn't believe it when they told me it had to go all the way up to Dr. Cardinal. I asked about it eight weeks ago."

"Well, it's dangerous," he says patiently, as if explaining to a toddler that no, you shouldn't put your hand in the bright thing floating on top of the candle.

Don't fucking patronize me, I almost say. "What do *you all* know about danger in here? Do you have *any idea* what I had to do to get here? I . . ." Blood leaps into my face. Part of me badly wants to tell him about the boar hunt, to establish my bona fides as not just a bleeding-heart do-gooder leading a judgily named club, but as a tracker, hunter, worker. But the other thing it establishes me as is, at least to them, a caveman, a brute — a Morlock again, stabbing things with sharpened sticks. They never do that here. And what do I want to prove to him, anyway? That I *am* one of those ferocious beasts the dome is meant to keep out, or that I'm *not*? "Look, I just think you guys need to recalibrate some. Just being outside of the buildings is hardly dangerous."

"People aren't used to it, though."

I raise my voice slightly in case the others are listening. "Back home, kids do this in grade five. When they're nine or ten years old. Does it seem *at all* weird to you that our degree is supposedly training people to go out and restore ecosystems, but doesn't train us on *actual* ecosystems? Just fake little tame ones?"

"Well, the scientific principles are the s—"

"Just saying if we *really* want to restore things, shouldn't we all be getting ready to, you know, get out into the world we're trying to restore?" That's bait again; I watch carefully to see who's nodding, who's smirking, who's looking away, who hasn't heard me. Supposedly these are the students — these ones right here in my program, environmental science — who are eager to rebuild the world that has been lost. They should be champing at the bit to get out of here. Instead, everyone is making unserious small talk with someone else. My stomach clenches with frustration and helplessness: Okay, so they're not interested in signing up for Share the Bounty. But this is what they're training for. This is it. What will they do if they don't leave this place?

"Anyway, I'm sure the kids enjoy it," St. Martin says awkwardly, sliding in the needles and catching himself with a yelp.

"Yeah. It's always a good time." I refrain from pointing out that we don't have the constructed wetland, the fake prairie, the meticulously planted parkland, we don't have any of the painstaking ecosystems generated here to let students see a baseline of what various ecosystems used to look like. What we've got is ancient textbooks and a river valley so close to dead most of the time that we can't even *do* this exercise every year. Sometimes the kids come back with no notes.

I wanted him to say something about leaving campus, which of course was the real reason I begged for us to get some outside fieldwork. I also wanted him to say something about the barrier around Howse, which I know we're approaching. And I already knew he wouldn't. No matter what else you can bait the insiders about, you cannot joke about the enclosure. In their world of walls and cells, everything separated from everything else, it is their greatest article of faith. It is not included in his definition of *danger*, instead it is what keeps him In Here, safe and completely divided from Out There.

Our snake of students slipslides downwards between larch and pine, then across a pretty clearing paved with flowers and tough-looking butterflies, and then we turn full-on to the sun and reach the spot I suggested in my message to Karina all those weeks ago: a small cold stream running east–west, and on either side of it, two gentle slopes therefore facing north and south. The sun is thin and clear in a cloudless sky of a blue so dark it verges on indigo.

She explains the exercise. I'm barely listening; I've done this one literally hundreds of times. Half the students monitor one side of the slope, half the other, then you go back and compare notes and see what the differences are in species diversity and numbers. That leads into the very basic conversation about sunlight, temperature, precipitation, runoff, nutrient retention, and soil formation, the knowledge we teach the kids is essential for growing food, which they already know is a matter of life or death. You can tell them in the classroom, of course. But it's better, so much better, to climb back up to campus, sweaty and triumphant, and compare lists, and watch the faces light up when they realize how different the two slopes can possibly be when they're so close together.

This is about muscle memory, although the species are new. I put myself in the centre of our group, and we move up the north slope of the tiny stream, pacing out one-metre grids. Without even hearing their accents you can tell at once who came to this place from somewhere else. A boy cries out in a panic as a whiskeyjack flutters towards his head, then straightens up and laughs self-consciously. On the other slope, a girl squeals as she gets too close to the stream and squelches into a wet spot; another girl hauls her out, smiling. Some of us are looking down, cataloguing plants and insects on our tablets; some of us are looking up nervously, only reassured by a glimpse of Karina. For subsistence living to work you need rules and regulations; I had thought there would be none here. But they don't need rules. They have this fear of the outside that works just as well. Or better.

Every time I hear *No one leaves here after they graduate*, I open my tablet, open the document I have named "1" to keep it at the top, and enter a tick-mark.

We are spreading out, and with that delicate, electrical-storm feeling of being in the right place at the right time, the sense of the hunter, I detach myself from the others and begin to climb, moving in silence on the needle-cushioned stone. I rehearse my answer for when I am eventually found: Saw a rare orchid. Had to go look. Saw a rare orchid, didn't think they grew up here; wasn't on the species list. Didn't realize I'd left the others behind. Sorry. Saw a rare orchid.

There is no path here. I glance behind myself occasionally to see if I am leaving a trail in the needles, seeing nothing, only my shadow black as ink in the strong sun hovering over me, stealthy and sure. When they find me I have to remember not to say I did nothing wrong. I must say only that I made a mistake. I did do something wrong, is what I must say.

As I climb, the voices below me fall away, and soon I am in true silence once more. The air is even getting cooler up here, though the sun is still full and bright, and stings my exposed face below my hat whenever I lift my head to check my bearings. The view is stupefying; it knocks you flat. And it reminds me again that there is no sign of human activity around this place, none at all, no roads, no buildings, no access of any kind. It is so perfectly isolated that there is not a chance that anybody could simply stumble across it by accident, and I imagine you can barely find it even if you do know what you're looking for.

As if on cue, I spot the barrier, with a light, full-body shock that plants me in place. It is like something from a recurring dream, half-remembered until it is before you, and then every detail from the depths of sleep clicks into place at once so that you cannot deny it any more. The old domes had their geometric slabs of transparent solids. But here, and only in full sunlight, I see the new one: a shimmer like heat haze, except with colours: blue and pink but both very faint, extending from near the ground to not quite the tops of the trees. I suspect that it goes up though, that it is a true dome, and I can only not see it because there is no contrast against the blue of the sky.

It should be humming. I can hear a hum from every device in my room. I can even hear my tablet hum. But it is silent. I stare and it seems to accept my stare like a statue of a deity, taking it as its due. Go on and stare, it says. You can do nothing to me. Maybe I'm imagining it.

Can I do *nothing* to it? What will it do to *me*?

There are no animals on campus bigger than a bird or a squirrel. For safety, they said. The orientation video. They tell you it's meant to keep out the dangerous wildlife, like bears and cougars — that it's essentially a type of electric fence. They don't need to say that, like any other electric fence, it works from either side. In theory students should have no trouble avoiding it, especially the 99 percent that never leave the built parts of campus. But I don't want to avoid it. I want to look.

I hear the footsteps long before their owner comes into view, and I'm already turning, skidding down the slope, almost colliding with St. Martin as he steps out from behind a tree, his hands out on either side as if he is trying to keep his balance on a sheet of ice. For a split second we are so close that I can see the hot blue ring around his dark irises, bright as a flame against the white sclera, and then we both take a large step backwards.

"Don't," he gasps first. "Don't touch it."

"In orientation they said it was meant to deter wildlife," I say. "It's set to give a little shock, right? It's not really dangerous."

"I . . . just don't touch it."

"Did they lie about it? Is that what you're trying to say?"

He holds up a hand for a pause, and catches his breath. He must have run up here, I realize. To get ahead of the others, or away from the others. "I'm not saying they *lied*. I'm saying it's . . . it's not *safe* for us to touch. Why on earth would anyone even want to?"

"You've never tested it?"

"Of course not!"

"So you just believe what they tell you?"

"Yes!"

"Bull*shit* this is for bears," I tell him. "It's for people. It's the last line in the defense of making sure people don't know where this place is. I bet it's set so high it'll kill any human who touches it."

"That can't be true."

"Why not?"

"I don't know what kind of people you think we . . ." He trails off, seeing my face, and chooses his next words more carefully. "Why do *you* think we don't want outsiders to know exactly where we are?"

"Because you're all cowards."

"That's not it. Think."

"Yes it is." I close the distance between us again. I'm trying not to yell at him, not to even raise my voice, because we'll get caught. "Any other answer you could give me is a variation on 'you're cowards.' You're all afraid of people. Afraid of everyone outside this place — because there's more of them than there are of you, and that is the only reason. That's what you're afraid of: being mobbed. That's why you only allow a handful of us to enroll every year. You think you'll be *swarmed*. And for what? Because you won't open your doors and share. Because you never have."

"Reid. Don't you think admin has tried it? In the past? What do you think happened?"

"What did they *tell you* happened?"

We glare at each other, panting in the thin and airless air, for far too long. His face is wretched with worry beneath its thin film of sweat. I don't care if I am asking too much of him. I don't care if this ends our friendship. I am standing upslope from him and this makes us almost the same height and if I threw a punch, a really good one, from my shoulder, it would hit him in a great spot, right in the philtrum. I used to win fights that way when I was a kid. Fighting for Henryk, usually, because he would just curl up instead of fighting back. St. Martin wouldn't fight back either.

Something inside me wavers and collapses, and it is so obvious that relief washes over his face. "Let's go back," he says.

"Is everyone looking for me?"

"No. Karina's over with the other group. Tanner was trying to catch fish in the stream and fell in."

I laugh despite myself, and clamp a hand over my mouth. On the way back down, I can't help it and ask, "Are you going to say anything? About me going up to look . . ."

"I . . . no. I mean technically you didn't break any rules." I can't see his face, as he's ahead of me, but I hear the reluctance in his voice. He *wants* to say something; his issue, I suspect, is that he cannot think of who to say anything to or what to say. I have plausible deniability on my side. Do we also have friendship? Are we friends? I don't know. He was the only one who noticed I was missing.

"Wait a minute," he says, "where are you going? This isn't the way we came."

"No, I can hear people just over there. It'll be quicker this way." The words are not even fully out of my mouth when I feel something shift under my feet. Not needles. Stone.

My body moves while my mind goes somewhere else. Already it is mourning something that hasn't happened yet. Or has happened in the past. A long, long time ago and someone's powerful hands pulling me from a mudslide. Looking up through the thick air to a face I knew, a face like mine, curls like mine. Hands lifting me into the safety of air.

I get one arm around a tree and the other on St. Martin, his flailing wrist, and though I feel bone and tendon twist under my hand, I'm not letting go, and nothing breaks. You would have to do worse than that for the bones of these people. Not like mine, breaking at a single bite. Life over limb, anyway. Isn't that what we teach the kids? Among other things?

Shouts of alarm downslope. A flurry of stone, dust, broken wood, an evergreen branch slapping me across the cheek so hard it leaves a perceptible residue of resin. They say when it gets hot enough here the trees go up like candles all on their own. Because of this accelerant they produce. Their own destruction coursing through their cells. Amazing.

It's over in a moment, and our tree has held, and the ground between me and St. Martin is at quite a drastic angle now, but he is so tall that my grip hasn't broken. Still it is a long time before I can let go, cautiously, leaving a visible dent around his wrist, and climb down, shaking with adrenaline, feeling it pour into my veins like the blood of trees, ready to catch fire.

His mouth is moving; I cannot hear him past the ringing in my ears. Even when I pitch forward from my tree and catch myself on the edge of the new cliff between us before I fly head over heels over it, our faces an inch apart, I cannot hear him. He grabs me under the armpits and pulls once, firmly, and sets me on my feet. Despite my jacket I can feel how cold his hands are.

Blood is pattering onto our shoes and pants, onto the needles below our feet, sudden as rain. "Jesus," I begin, "are you —" but he's closing his long fingers around my wrist, shouting over my head.

I've sliced my hand open on a stone, and for just a second before the pain hits I'm impressed at how clean the cut is — as if somewhere, a hundred millennia ago, some ancient ancestor is nodding at the performance of the flint knife he's chipped.

It's opened a doorway in my palm where I must have caught my full weight on the edge, and through the oozing blood I see the lines of muscle like a butchered rabbit, and something else: purple and blue and green and black, the trees, the spiraling arms of them, still in me, of course they are still in me, I knew they were not gone, only sleeping, but now exposed, breathing the thin wild air just like the rest of us, still there, still inside me, still in me — *it's you it's you it's you it's you you're awake it's you no don't wake up don't don't it's moving I can see it moving*

I don't black out but it's a fight, my knees buckling, not at the pain, not at the blood, just at this reminder that I still live with the adversary, that the killer is still in the house, the silent companion who will never leave me.

Then the darkness lifts and in the day's ordinary brightness restored Karina is at my side, gasping, clucking, and I'm fending off St. Martin's praise at how my quick thinking saved his life. He wasn't going to die, it was just a little rockslide. Clean white bandages with a tiny *HU* logo in blue go around and around, hiding the monster from view, and not a word is said about where I was or where I was supposed to be.

Is this what you were so afraid of that you glassed yourself off from the world? You were afraid of this? Me, us?

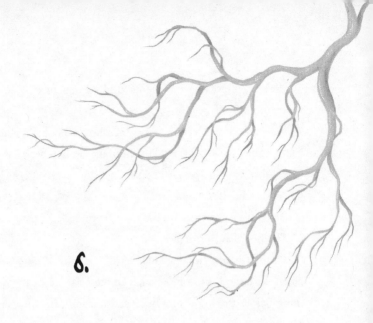

6.

I left everyone behind and I said I'd come back. I said, *No one else has ever come back, but I'll come back*. Maybe I didn't say it out loud. I wrote my best and oldest friend a letter — my best and oldest friend who survived. It feels like forever ago. In it I meant to say to him, *It should have been her here, Nadiya*. It should have been her and it both galls me that that's the case, and it hurts me that she isn't alive and here instead of me. Not only out of the three of us but out of all of us that we knew, it *should have been her* in this place. She should have been the one person who achieved escape velocity and flew as good as to the stars — to a place as remote and inescapable as any space station or Mars colony. In the letter I said none of it. I said other things.

Behind me, Clementine says, "I want a big mad giant breakfast, you know? Like two breakfasts in one, but different breakfasts. How do we get that? What are you writing?"

"It's in one of the sub-menus under Preferences. Letter to my mom."

She hovers over my shoulder, then heads for the kitchen. "You got nice writing. I think I'm one of the last kids back home that still knows cursive. We had the one lady — Mrs. Petruzzi. Only one still insisting on teaching it. Then she died. Five years and nobody else stepped up. You want anything?"

"Coffee? Lots of sugar?"

"Sure you don't wanna come with?" she coaxes as she sets down the mug. "Everyone's gonna be there. It's kinda the big thing before the big thing. Because it's semifinals. Spartans versus Spirit."

"I'll catch up with you guys. Just got a few things to finish."

"St. Martin will be there!"

"Yeah, he goes to all these things. Wait. What's *that* supposed to mean?"

"Nothing!" She holds her hands up defensively, making me laugh, then adds, "It'll be completely dead here. What're you gonna do instead?"

"I . . . nothing. Just walk around."

I shouldn't have hesitated. She watches me closely for several seconds, lightly suspicious, unsure. "You can tell me anything, you know."

"I know that, Clementine, honestly. I just need to stretch my legs. That's all!"

When she is gone, I put my watch in my desk, admiring the tan line it leaves behind, and my tracker necklace too — darkened, no blinking light, but a lot of us still wear it under our clothes like a good-luck talisman. The watch almost certainly tracks our locations (no one talks about it — it is one of those assumed things, I think, like the single rooms), and I have little faith that the tracker in the necklace has truly been disabled.

The tablet I debate for a while, then I put that in my desk too. I would like to have the camera on it, but it's fragile, probably the most valuable thing I could now call mine.

I dress in my old clothes, the ones I wore here. They seem impossibly shabby and shameful now, aside from being spattered in blood and less savoury things, and I hold them in my hands for a long time, because you have to feel the size and shape and heft of something before it becomes known to you, before you can understand it and how to carry it. The trousers spun from plastic yarn, the undershirt and overshirt, the ancient hand-me-down wool coat with its remade buttons, the plastic-soled rabbit-skin boots. I tighten the straps of my rucksack, and step out into the cool autumn light.

For what I have in mind the easiest way through campus is north, down the smaller avenues where the grey stone walls crowd so closely you can stretch out your arms on either side and touch them. I pass the spires of the water treatment plant, gurgling and humming like a contented baby, and a dozen vat centres, some of them warming the surrounding air to a damp, tropical heat, like the inside of the botanical gardens. No faces track me from the windows. It is Sunday morning, and there are no classes, and there is a big game, and everyone not at the game is sleeping in.

Even to myself I am not sure what I want to do, except see if it's possible to pass through that barrier. This time I also don't know what excuses I might give when I get caught, because I expect to be caught. There *seem* to be no rules written against it, but you can break unwritten ones no problem. Last night when we were all sitting in the quad watching for meteors, I thought about telling St. Martin the story of my coming here — not the steamcart, not the mountains, but before that. Because we were sitting apart from the others, because they were not listening. Because every time he spoke he turned towards me, instead of, like me, speaking while facing the same way and not moving. Are we really friends? Can we be friends if I feel so certain that he would turn me in for doing this? Clementine wouldn't.

Behind the last building, as they quite sensibly designed it, there's a drastic slope — nearly vertical. No path in the stone, no steps. Only stubborn scrub, slippery lichen and moss, and a faint mist drifting from a concealed waterfall nearby. I am unsurprised and undismayed, and I climb, carefully, my dirty clothes camouflaged against the stone.

Yesterday afternoon I got another shot against my Cad, the sixth since I came here. Dr. Gibson watched me closely, taking notes as I chattered away, as always. The other students, I have slowly come to realize, get a nurse; I always get Gibson himself. This is routine now. I have questions for him. He expects them. But I will not ask, because there are things I would prefer he not know that I'm thinking about. Sometimes I worry my evasion is telling him anyway: the absence of certain words crafted from the shape of those words I do say, their negative image making a perfect shape of what I'm trying to hide. He always seems to be on the verge of saying something anyway — maybe answering one of those questions I haven't asked — but he stops himself too. We talk about other things; we speak in parallel to one another's conversations, not perpendicular.

I climb. My ears are ringing from nerves, adrenaline, only. Dr. Gibson says I'm not anemic any more. He says I'm doing very well. Healthy as a horse. I've never seen a horse. They all died. We still say it. We still say *as good as gold*, when none of us have held gold or know its goodness. I climb and I don't mind the thin air. The mountain still rears above me, infinite, no summit visible from here. Sometimes I even have to pause and press my face to the stone, feel the thrumming in it.

At home I was never alone. Emotionally, mentally, and also physically it was like being a spider in some great communal web, feeling at all times the threads moving under my feet, even asleep. Here I am alone constantly. Everyone is. I feel numb, cut off from humanity. Sometimes I think I need this: or else I cannot discover who I am. Because we cannot do so in the collective, only in the individual. Sometimes I think this is the worst thing that has ever happened to me and I will never recover. But this is how they all live here, this is how they *want* to live.

For a second I freeze: nothing deliberate about it, just sheer animal nervousness, at a sound behind me. The crackle and hiss of needles, slow and calculated. Run? Fight? Lie?

Lying sounds great, and I'm turning, lining up all my excuses neatly as a column of files in my tablet, and then I see Clementine struggling up the slope towards me.

She's changed her skirt for a pair of much-bepocketed baggy pants, like me, and her dress shoes for runners. I let her get close, then grab her so she can sit for a minute on the stone next to me. We look at each other, eyebrows raised. Conversational chicken.

"What are you doing?" she says first.

"Why did you follow me?"

"Why do you *think* I followed you?"

This is going to go on for days, I think, and then I laugh — partly at the thought of them finding our skeletons up here, dead from a decade of questions that we answered with more questions, and partly because I'm actually relieved to not be alone. And relieved that it's *her*, specifically. "I wanted to go look at the barrier," I tell her. "And see if I can go through it."

She purses her lips. "Sounds like a good way to get killed."

"It does sound like it. But I'm pretty damn sure that's just what they're telling us. Like how when the kids back home are little there's always someone telling them there's a Boogeyman who stalks the hallways, so they shouldn't leave their rooms at night . . ."

"Mm. For us it's Mother Phaedra. Same basic idea though." She gets up, dusting herself down, and pulls me up. "Well, let's go see if the Boogeyman is real."

"Look, there's no need for both of us to get in trouble. You should go back."

"Nope. You shouldn't go alone. Not safe."

I'm right and she's right; we silently agree to leave it at that, and begin to climb again, boosting and tugging one another over the trickier angles of stone. After about an hour we can see it again — the enclosure. St. Martin struggled to explain it when I kept nagging him: *It is both physical and not physical. Like a wall?* I demanded. *Like lightning? No, no, like . . . It's a real thing, though, right? It's not just energy. Yes, it's real, and it's . . . no, it's a field, it's like a field of particles suspended in . . . something. Electricity? Not exactly. A form of energy. Look, I don't know. You'd have to ask one of the physics people.*

I can't see what he's talking about. There is only that subtle difference — the slight change in colour, less so in shape, size — of the world on this side of the barrier and that side. Clementine snorts, unimpressed. "Doesn't look like much."

"Yeah, people say that about things, and then next thing they know they're dead."

"That's true," she admits.

As I approach it I test myself for fear as if I am assaying a sample in one of my chemistry classes and I find only anticipation, excitement. I try to remember the other times in my life I've felt it. Not simple terror, not anxiety. Everything in my life at home I did out of fear and never realized it. Digging in the dirt for fear of starving. Carrying spears for fear of wild dogs. Smothering Henryk for fear of being alone . . .

It doesn't feel solid to my outstretched hand. It does feel like what St. Martin talked about — strange particles suspended in an even stranger matrix, linked to each other with energies not like the tame lightning from our solar cells or the understandable fusion of the sun. Something else.

At first it does feel like fear, anxiety. A roiling in the stomach, a cry from all my cells wailing *Go back! Go back!* Or is it Clementine? No, she's standing behind me, anxious but not stopping me.

I push, keep pushing, arms out, and the anxiety turns into pain: an oddly familiar, long-remembered pain. The pain along every nerve, pain like fire but still less strong than my determination, pain exactly like that of Cad. The feeling visible as whiteness, as light. Still I cannot see the barrier. I seem to walk through the empty air. Then real force, as if I am walking through a wall. My nose deforms, my lips, I feel it and this time I almost do retreat.

A roaring in the ears and nothingness. I am through. A new world has given itself to me because it had no choice.

For a moment no one else is on the far side of this thing but me. Not for who even knows how far around us. I am the only one. I want to shout, roar, whoop; I feel five years old, king of the castle. Instead I straighten, dust down my clothes, passionlessly note the freshly melted edges of lapel and sleeve, *that* can't be good, and turn to help Clementine get through — her teeth bared in pain, eyes huge.

As one, we turn and look back at the barrier from this side: still invisible. Still that hum that hangs just at the edge of sensation rather than hearing, just a little too subtle to activate the bones in the ear. "Holy shit," she says. "They didn't mention *that* at orientation. Now what, smart guy?"

I shrug. "I want to get the lay of the land. Look around. Maybe work on a map — no, don't give me that look, I didn't bring my tablet! And you better not have brought yours. What's in all those pockets, anyway? And I want to find something else, I don't know. Like . . ."

"Like a trophy," she suggests, eyes sparkling. "Come back with a moose skull, act casual about it."

I guffaw, cover my mouth. Can you *imagine*. But she's onto something, I think. "I don't think moose live up this high," I tell her. "But I bet elk do. What if we stalked an elk?"

"Jesus."

"You don't see them much down in Calgary, do you?"

"No," she says slowly. "No, people said they've been moving north for a long time."

"An elk." I nod magisterially, as if I have given a royal decree. Something dangerous — that's what I want as a trophy. Not to kill. Just to find. To prove I can still do it. Plus, it's the rut, and it will be nearly impossible to sneak up and look, which is half the point. And I can map while I do it; and then come back. "Come on."

The air smells the same outside the barrier and I laugh at myself for thinking it would be different. As juicy as a ripe cherry — always a wonder, even though I should be used to it by now. Not like home, with its constant faint undertones of burning trash and top notes of compost. This smell, I understand, comes from the humidity and the living trees. It is their unshed blood I smell, molecules of it coming out through the needles. As I go, I touch the branches of the larch, oddly soft, like fur. Clementine moves behind me in gratifying silence.

Why an elk? Because an elk can kill you like anything else up here, and people think it can't, just because it is not a predator. Because an elk *wants* to kill you during the rut. Because I want to see, up close, something that can kill me, and not get killed. Because there's no rule against it.

We move quietly, watching for signs — also of cougar and bear, because those still survive up here. Everywhere else in the province they are long gone, killed for food or because they attacked those precious few livestock still left. Entire ecosystems collapsed from the tiniest prey to the largest predator, and up here it is still precarious — nothing with sharp enough teeth will show the slightest compunction about eating me or Clementine. I imagine only they would be a little depressed about it. So ropy, so short. So bony. And this awful taste . . . as if the meat were tainted with mould . . .

Half a hoofprint is enough. It snaps everything else into focus. The edges of branches and the bitten edges of shrubs where the elk have browsed, the hint of a trail where their greater weight has pressed down the vegetation. Individual hairs glinting in the sunlight, caught here and there on the trees. I am in a living place. I wonder when it will stop feeling strange. I am in a living place, not a place that is dead, or only barely, weakly stirring as it attempts to resurrect its desiccated corpse.

I could stay here. I *should* stay here. Shouldn't I? A place where everything is bursting with life?

In silence I point down to the hoofprint, and Clementine nods, and we go on. The whiskeyjacks follow us — some silently, staring, and some calling out in alarm. I like their eyes, like black chips of stone, and the pertness of their short dark beaks. They seem less overtly predatory than their magpie cousins. They flit from tree to tree and watch us from behind the different greens, like me, hungry for new things, curious as I am.

I feed the whiskeyjacks bits of the food I've brought, laughing at their tameness as they swoop down to take it from my hand — crackers, cheese, sesame-coated dried peas, toasted nuts. Everything with lots of salt. Clementine didn't bring anything, not counting on a daytrip, so I feed her too. One bird bolder than the rest lands briefly on my thumb, snatches a cashew, flees. A little dinosaur. I feel lightheaded, exhilarated. There is no one here but us and the animals. No adversary within me. I no longer walk with the enemy. Is this the first time I've really felt it? In my bones?

Late in the afternoon we find a shallow stream, clear as glass, so transparent I can see the fish inside it preserved as if inside a museum exhibit. Only when I stare can I see them moving minutely, swimming against the current to stay in place, their gills moving and tails moving and almost nothing else. Following some perverse impulse I lie flat on the bank, feeling the dampness move up through my clothes.

"Girl, what are you *doing*?"

"Look, this is gonna work." And anyway, I have no idea. I extend an arm slowly till my fingertips meet the surface of the water, then make a wild snatch at the closest fish.

The cold is a shock. The living animal in my hand is more of a shock, and I fumble it onto the grass, stunned. Today feels like a day when everything I set my hand to succeeds. The fish is like a beautiful statue of glass — I've never seen one alive, only the preserved specimens back home, colourless and stinking in their alcohol jars, or flat pictures in books. It is so intensely bright and lovely that it seems like a made thing, like each scale had to be crafted under a microscope and fitted into place with tweezers. One hot eye stares up at me so brightly it is as if it has a light fitted behind it, as if you could read by it. A trout, but I can't remember which one. We are both gasping for a moment; then both our breaths still. Clementine laughs, breathless too, startled.

"Do you want some?" I ask her.

"Hell no."

The whiskeyjacks are ecstatic about the guts. I fillet the thing inexpertly and dabble a piece of the sunrise-red flesh in the stream to rinse off the blood. If you kill something you shouldn't waste it, and if you don't intend to eat it you shouldn't kill it. Which everybody knows.

They say there was still fish sometimes in the river when I was a child, now and then. Fish farming, too, had been tried decades before, and failed for lack of water, like so much else. This is what I would explain to St. Martin, if I felt I could talk to him like this. Maybe he would be the ambassador to the rest of Howse. To say that we were not lazy or stupid out there — that *everything* you could think of doing to arrest the fall had been done. That the people who came before us confidently burned their metaphorical boats, then discovered that there was no wood to build new ones.

And don't you think we knew that? Don't you think we knew what was happening? How can you look me in the eye and say *You've never eaten fish?* with any kind of surprise?

I am breathless for a moment, as if I have actually been arguing with someone — with St. Martin, with whom I have never even brought this up. My hand shakes as I lift the little piece of flesh to my mouth. They cannot do this back home. None of this they can do. Look at this water, like glass.

I'm not who I was there. I am new, something else, someone else. I am free. I am at the top of the known world and I must take off everything that I used to be and throw it from a stone summit. I will leave all of that behind: all that dirt and smoke, all that hunger, thirst, all those small-minded people, all those people who stay inside, stay behind, all of that I renounce. I am not an insect shedding its exoskeleton into a new instar identical in shape to the old one but I am undergoing metamorphosis: breaking down to become something entirely new.

The piece of flesh is so cold from its brief bath in the stream that for a moment I can only imagine I've put a piece of ice in my mouth. Then the heat of my tongue warms it and for several longer and much stranger seconds it is as if there is a second tongue on top of mine — the same softness, texture, a wet velvetiness. I am more startled than enraptured, but I recover, and chew, and swallow.

If Henryk were here, if we were still the children we once were, we would agree that this was the magic potion from the story where a witch can transform you into all things.

Henryk is not here. He belongs to a past I have left behind. He is like my Cad. And my fear. And my worry and my cowardice.

I wash my hands in the water, not wanting to smell like fish blood, and nod to Clementine, and we go on.

The sun is almost down when I see it, and I war internally between declaring this a *Yes, you did it* and a *No, you didn't, you're too far* for a long time. But the buck stands still for ten seconds, fifteen, twenty. At a minute, I detach myself from behind the outcropping of stone and slink towards it, staying low, beckoning for Clementine to follow me. My heart is pounding. Is hers? Can they hear that? Prey animals have senses like you can't even imagine. A whole different world than the one we live in. It's a miracle we manage to kill any at all. I wonder when this elk last saw a human. Maybe it never has.

I move when the trees rustle in the wind, making the same sound as when the wind hits my clothes. The light is low and golden. My shadow is as long as a tree. I am part of this whole landscape, I am outside the perimeter, I remind myself. If I wanted to go anywhere, anywhere in the whole world, I could do that. If.

The elk is enormous. I had hugely underestimated his size. Up close, he sails past impressive and into magisterial. And threatening too, and for some reason worse because he is standing so still, scenting the wind. He looks charged-up with potential energy, as if the longer he stands there, the more he is collecting, so that when he moves it will be with terrifying speed. His ruff is so thick it looks as if he has killed a grizzly to hang around his neck.

I also think I thought his antlers would be blunt. They are not. He has adorned himself with knives.

They were right, back home. I have come to this place of danger. I have left safety and come to danger with open arms.

He is beautiful. He is like the god of the mountains. What would our god be back home? A mangy rabbit, a sickly feral dog?

I glance behind myself quickly to make sure that Clementine is still there, and that I have an escape route that is clear of obstacles and the motion alerts him to my presence. Still in silence, he takes a step towards us. His head goes down, his eyes flare like candle flames. Still in silence. Then he snorts, a sharp, frightening sound that hits me in the pit of my stomach. Takes another step towards us. And another. We are unmoving. We are not a threat. Please don't charge.

He stops. I stop. I did not come to worship you, I want to tell him, and I don't want it to sound like a plea, like I am pleading for my life. I want him to see us as equals. Only to look. I mean neither worship nor blasphemy. Don't kill me. There's a whole world I need to change.

The sun is going down. I back away from him, hiding in the dimness, in the scarlet darkening to indigo, and only

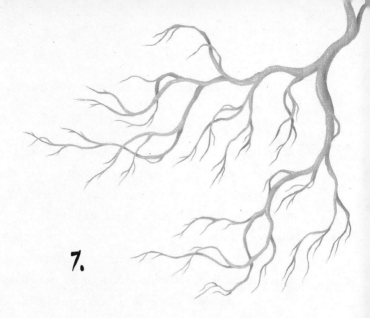

7.

"Thank God we're *finally* off probation. Weird that they gave you a week longer than me, huh? Which skirt should I pick?"

"They said *I* was the negative influence. That one on the end." I point, and Clementine pulls it from the rack: long, plain blue, with the discreet stylized *H* of the logo near the hem, glittering in silver thread. I'm used to her asking strings of questions you have to answer in order.

"This is frumpy, girl. I'm not in *Little House on the Prairie*."

"It's December!"

"We won't be *outside*. There's a pedway that goes straight from here to the hall. This one." She pulls out another skirt, almost a belt, blue and white tartan with a much bigger logo. "What are you going to wear?"

"I'm not going."

"But we're off probation!"

"Yes, but . . ."

"Don't tell me you're gonna run off on your own *again*. Don't even *start*."

Clementine busies herself rummaging through our closet and speculating on whether you could just order some party clothes and how long it might take to create them from the vats, our benevolent bacterial quartermasters. I drink my coffee, luxuriating in the milk and sugar on my tongue, focusing on that.

Probation doesn't mean anything here; it sounded punitive, it made me think of some kind of incarceration — it made me think I would have a probation officer, which I read about once. All it meant was that we both had a *P* next to our names in our tablets, on the kitchen screen, wherever we appeared in the system — messages to friends, anything like that. Then I was merely mystified. The locals clearly thought it was a big deal, that *P*, since it would go on my permanent transcript. But what did a permanent transcript mean in a world where transcripts barely existed? It would be like climbing a mountain to find the wise man at the top and insisting that he show his Wise Man of the Mountain License.

In theory, the *P* also meant that I was not permitted to attend sporting events or social gatherings, and again in practice I hadn't been going to those anyway; it angered Clementine a lot more than me. I was still allowed to run Share the Bounty, for what little that was worth — the year is almost over and all I've accomplished so far is signing up a handful of people for meetings to discuss lobbying university administration to back our group. Nothing concrete yet. In the beginning we, mostly I, talked about starting satellite campuses in the cities, doing food drops, starting seed libraries with their modified seedstock, helping build irrigation systems, drilling wells . . . but it was all talk, and I suspected it would remain all talk.

"You should wear this one too." Clementine points at the same skirt on my side of the closet. "Show off your legs."

"Everybody knows what legs look like."

"You know what I mean. What if someone signs up for your group when they see you dressed up for once?"

"Not the quality of recruit I was hoping for."

She snorts affectionately, and turns back to the closet. "Hmm. Long sleeves, short skirt. You're lucky your Cad didn't fuck up your skin, you know. You should see some of the folks back home. They look like they've been pushed through a metal screen."

"Us too." I put my cup on the table next to my bed and curl up, tucking my legs under me. "You know Cad is half the reason I'm pushing for them to open their gates. All the lives that they could save but also all the . . . all the eyes, the fingers, the toes. The bodies. The strength. How are sick people supposed to rebuild anything?"

"You don't have to preach to me," she says patiently, her head buried in clothes. "It's just, you know. It's the way you're doing it. Like you know better than them. They don't like that. Maybe if you did it their way, followed the procedures or whatever . . . you know they like procedures."

"They don't have one for this. I keep asking if there's something I can follow. They let me talk about food drops and irrigation planning, but they refuse to talk about Cad. There isn't one single argument that they listen to."

"Well, there's probably a good reason for that."

"There isn't," I retort, more loudly than I intend. She goes still for a moment, then continues rummaging.

We had been almost all the way back to Prentice Hall when we were caught. And so politely too — not the way the Red Flags arrest someone back home, binding their hands so quickly, getting their feet off the ground so they can't run. A security guard dressed in a blue and white uniform like everybody else's, with the addition of a small metallic badge, touched my elbow and in an apologetic voice asked if we'd like to come with him as Dr. Cardinal wanted to have a little chat with us. We moved down the milky streetlit alley in absolute serenity, like swans floating down a river of light.

Of course we had set off alarms — one going out, and one coming in. *Why didn't you come after us when we triggered the first one?* I had asked, and Cardinal watched me for several seconds with her golden eyes, not hostile, mildly curious, as if this were something she had never been asked.

"Because we knew you would come back, and waiting was safer for our staff than leaving campus."

She didn't ask what we had been doing out there. She asked me whether we had communicated with anyone — verbally or by handing off a physical message. I began to say that it shouldn't matter, since we were allowed to mail letters out anyway, then trailed off while Clementine was much more loudly decrying this as a ridiculous idea. Were they reading our mail? Was that why it didn't matter?

Because we knew you would come back.

Because where else would I go? I had come here to do a job. Wouldn't I stay and do it? Of course.

I look down at my hands on the cotton blanket: tanned, scratched, and with no trace of the disease whatsoever. Nothing even so prominent as a washed-off inkstain. It drew in all its tendrils and went to sleep, like some undersea beast retreating to a tiny crack in a stone. Every month we put it to sleep again. Like in a fairy story.

"Why do *you* think people don't leave this place after they graduate?" I ask Clementine.

She emerges from the closet, thrusting her hair off her face. "I think you're overthinking this," she says. "There's no grand conspiracy or anything. Why don't they leave? Because it's nice here. Because you have the Childcare Centre for your kids, and the Elder House for Grandma and Grandpa. Because here they'll live long enough to become Grandma and Grandpa. Because there's water, there's food, there's electricity, there's . . . all this. Everything. How could you go back to shitting in a pot, dying of Cad, and starving for six months a year, after four years of this?"

"We weren't *starving*," I begin, but she's not wrong about the rest. "Are you going to go back?"

"Of course I am. When I can help people by going back."

"But what will you do after graduation if you don't leave here?"

"Same thing as everyone else. Work. Probably teach." She shrugs.

"Did you know that . . . that Howse is in touch with the other universities? I mean, the other . . . the other bunkers like this."

"No, I didn't know that. Makes sense though."

"St. Martin told me. It's how they keep everything balanced with students and staff — like an exchange program. It's almost like . . . what I keep thinking of is the old British empire. Their big argument was that they needed the resources from all the places they colonized. But they admitted right out loud that there were places they put their flag on that had nothing they wanted. They just . . . they just wanted their name on it. So I keep going back and forth, like . . . is that what I'm asking them to do? Put their flag on things? Say they've come to, I don't know, share their superior civilization and build some train tracks and some trains and then make the trains run on time? Is that horrible? What if that's what people want? Does that justify them overstepping once they start? If they ever start? I mean, I have to think about what my role is in this."

"Uh-huh." She's not listening. I sigh, and watch her primp and fuss as best she can with the standard clothing options and with the makeup she got from Feathers, the campus everything store. It's not quite four o'clock and the sun is almost entirely down. A week till the solstice and the slow return of light. On the back wall of our room, two rectangles of sunset pink flare for a moment against the white wall, then fade. Do I want to be alone here on such a dark night? Both yes and no. "Wait a minute," I tell her, as she returns from the bathroom for the last time to grab her tracker necklace.

"What? Is it my hair?"

"Is there going to be booze?"

"Oh hell yeah. And not like the little — you know. Fill out a million forms and watch the ice in your drink melt, like at Harlequin," she says, referring to the student bar, one of exactly two places on campus you're allowed to buy alcohol, in strictly measured doses from a single counter. (The other is the staff bar, where students aren't allowed.)

I waver again, and finally shrug. "Okay. I'm coming with you. Give me five minutes to get dressed."

Whenever you go to someone's room there's music playing, ours included (I myself have developed a taste for oldies from the '30s and '40s, like Fever of Wonder, R3fug3, and Aria the Envoy), so I am expecting the songs over the speakers when we enter the hall. I'm not expecting the volume, or the crowd — it seems like every student on campus is here, which can't be right, or it would be ten thousand people. In reality it must just be a couple hundred, but we're all packed in tight, a real sea of white and blue. Someone squeals and embraces Clementine when we come in, then shrugs and hugs me too — a moment of long hair brushing across my face like a cold breeze, lips briefly on my cheek. "You made it!" she cries.

The overhead lights are off, but the room is hotly lit with strings of smaller bulbs that change colour through the spectrum, tangled across the ceiling and dangling down the walls like ivy. Faces light up for a moment and vanish, or parts of faces: a bright blue nose, a red eye, flare of green across a cheekbone. I am bathed in sound and light. Clementine vanishes at once, of course, and I head towards the back of the hall where I think I can vaguely see a bar or a buffet or something.

This specific celebration, I'm given to understand, caps off classes for the year; next week is exams, and then we are off till March, when the new year starts. The atmosphere is joyous and relieved and even a little wild. It isn't that they don't celebrate here. It's that they don't *gather*. Everyone is soaking in a potent stew of pheromones that we all happily deny the existence of, because we are humans, and humans are above that.

I think for a moment of the school dances we had growing up — small, sedate affairs in the same place we normally had our weekend market. All the stalls pushed to one side, candles flickering in the underground space, their flames reflecting on the black slate floor, transforming the faces of all the kids I saw day in and day out: warm, flushed, nervous. Henryk and Nadiya dancing awkwardly, only touching with their fingertips, because *Ew, boys. Ew, girls.*

I shove the memory down and spot a familiar form at the back of the line for the bar, so I join it too and tap him on the shoulder. St. Martin turns, and smiles both in recognition and, I sense, at my outfit — the same as his. Blue blazer, white T-shirt, tight blue trousers. Clementine had urged me to dress up but the best I could do was pick something comfortable and accept her application of eyeliner and lipstick.

"They had a dress shirt," I say over the music; he leans down to listen. "With a tie. How come you didn't wear that?"

"How come *you* didn't?"

"I don't know how to tie a tie."

"I would have tied it for you," he says firmly, and he nudges me ahead of him as we reach the bar — a portable kitchen unit decorated with more of the dangling lights, and a young woman in white carefully supervising the addition of the actual alcohol to the mixers supplied by the unit. "What are you having?"

"I don't know."

"Two screwdrivers," he says, and hands me a glass as we wander back to join his friends. "This isn't your first time drinking, is it? Clementine says she used to booze it up starting from age ten back home."

"It's not my first time." I sip the drink, which just tastes like orange juice, and park myself at his elbow as the others chatter about some series they're all watching — separately, I realize, in their rooms, syncing up the presentation on their tablets. There's an emperor, a false emperor, a loyal body double for the emperor, a disloyal one, two good wives, three scheming wives, a concubine who believes herself to be in love with the real emperor and is unaware that her lover is the disloyal body double, and all of them are attempting to gain control of a magical stone orb hidden in the heart of some mountain. I feel hurt, for just a second, that they're devoting so much time and energy to analyzing the intricate plot of this long-defunct show, when if they would just take *one minute* to read about my group I could . . .

"It's Reid, right?" A small shadow detaches itself from behind a much taller boy and moves beside me: the red-haired girl I saw my first day but not since. Her face, like mine, has healed from the ordeal of getting here; she looks flushed and healthy, and does not appear to be working on her first drink. "I'm Hendrix. I heard you . . . um . . . is it true what they're saying?"

Oh, going through the barrier? *That* little thing? "It's true."

She smiles, pleased to confirm it. "What were you doing? Everyone has a theory. I thought it might be some kind of, you know . . . vision quest or something."

"Some kind of what?"

"You know. You fast, and then you go into . . . into the wilderness. And then you see things that tell you about your future." She reaches up to scratch her head, misses, and absentmindedly runs her nails along the sleeve of the boy next to her. "And I think you get . . . an animal? A vision of your . . . guardian animal."

"Sounds interesting, but no."

"And then Thorsten said it was —"

"Anyway, how are classes going?" I interrupt her, brightly.

"You're Reid Graham, aren't you?" someone else says, cutting in between us — a pale boy with dark hair, drinking something out of his translucent plastic cup that has stained his lips an undead violet colour. From his accent I think he is a

Howse local. I brace myself for the obvious, which he delivers. "You're the one trying to get some kind of . . . delegation. Together. To what . . . make admin send out missionaries? Or something? Drop care packages on the rest of the world?"

"Something like that." I'm not very interested in being baited, but he wants to hunt, and nothing would give him more pleasure than bringing down a self-appointed chosen one. I didn't appoint myself, asshole, I want to tell him; *they're* the ones who sent the acceptance letter. You got in just by being born here. I watch him closely. In the old days I would have wondered how to make an ally out of him. Now I see only a drunk boy with no filter. Back home you save everything because it might be useful; here, you jettison it right away for something better. I have no use for this boy.

"They've had the same time as us to figure things out," he insists, leaning closer; his breath is heavy and sweet. "And all the dropped blocks in the world . . . it's not our fault they never figured out how to put things back together. Everything's still there. Waiting to be picked up again."

"You've never left this place. How would you know?"

"Everybody knows. Look it up. There's pictures and video and . . . so *what* if I've fucking never left this place? What's that even supposed to mean? What's so great about out there? It's full of people like you."

"And now here we are," I tell him pleasantly, swirling the ice at the bottom of my cup. "In here. With you."

"That's enough," Hendrix snaps. "I thought we were friends, Taggart."

"You, I can be friends with. Her . . ."

"She's trying to help people!"

"She's trying to help *her* people," another girl says, pushing her long hair over her shoulder so it doesn't dabble in her drink. "I read her little manifesto or whatever. Not even deciding who needs help, just saying we should give those people everything and see what happens. Like throwing a box of tools into an anthill and expecting them to build a house." She laughs prettily. Somehow she has coordinated a tank top and a long skirt into something that looks like a ballgown. She is a princess at the feast, her attitude says; I am an unwanted guest. A peasant that slipped in somehow.

"So you're saying you're the kind of person who would watch someone fall and step over them because you think they'll get up on their own," I say. "Right? Where you're going is more important. They clearly weren't trying to get anywhere. Were they. And they can't possibly be hurt."

"I *think* you're being a little oversensitive. Especially for someone who, in this childish metaphor of yours, did walk away."

St. Martin takes my arm. "Let's go get another drink," he says. "And something to eat." He turns to the princess. "It doesn't matter, Madeline. If you want to say I told you so about something, you have to do it *after* someone tries and fails, not before."

The hall is so crowded and therefore so hot that when we step outside for some fresh air it feels like being slapped in the face, even though it's actually not that cold — at worst, a few degrees below freezing. It smells like it wants to snow, and I gasp the air, hungry for that scent after all the dancing bodies and spilled drinks. In the last few hours I've had a lot of food, mostly snacks, but also several boozy beverages; St. Martin has been doing the same, but we finally declared ourselves done and got two mugs of hot chocolate with the intent of drinking it outside. I am warm with alcohol and humiliation and rage but it all feels very far away, and I am almost enjoying it — the warmth and the dizziness and the bright sparkly edges on everything.

A bench is situated invitingly by the doors, but there's also a large flat rock, and I sit on that instead and cross my legs, uncaring whether I get dirt on my pants. They're not my pants anyway. Nothing here belongs to me and I should never have expected it to. I came here with nothing — no, not nothing. Only the dirty little remnants of my people, not even brought as offerings to the gods that live here on Mount Olympus but something I had to hide. I have not even put up my magpie painting. It's crude daubs compared to what I can pull up in two seconds on my tablet.

"I did walk away," I say, blowing on the surface of my mug. My hands are shaking but not enough to spill. All I can seem to focus on is the distance between the top of the mug and the top of the liquid. "I walked away saying I'd get help. I said it's only four years. And when I come back I'll know so much — I'll change everything, you'll see. I didn't know nobody comes back. Why doesn't anybody come back? I never knew. Now I know."

St. Martin is silent; he lifts his cup, but doesn't drink, and then puts it back down on his lap. He has taken the bench, so we are a few feet apart. But it's so quiet out here I can still hear him when he replies, "You know, this isn't real chocolate. Like the coffee and tea. It's . . . a collection of molecules meant to replicate the real thing. We wouldn't know if it's close enough. It's been generations since someone would have tasted it and been able to tell. Because they tasted the real thing."

"So what."

"So when you told me about . . . about the books you read. Back home. And how you always wondered what it was like to eat a piece of chocolate, or drink a cup of coffee . . . well, we're the same. We're more advanced at faking things, that's all. Out there you're eating real food. You're doing real work. In here . . ."

"So I shouldn't have come. I should have stayed where things were real."

"That's not what I'm saying!" He half rises from the bench, then sits again, a gawky mantis gleaming under the street lights above us. Inside the building, a great cheer goes up for something — I couldn't hear what. The music gets louder. "Look, I'm saying . . . You've never said it out loud but you think we're . . . weak, we've been locked away too long, something's atrophied. I know you think that. I'm amazed we've become friends despite it. You have this theory that we're accepting people from outside to get fresh genes in, to strengthen a weak bloodline. Maybe we are! I don't know. I don't know why they accept the students they do. I truly don't. But at the same time, outside here is a world of . . . of danger and instability and turmoil. And you're asking people from *here* to go out *there* and fix it. I mean, wouldn't you expect them to be a little hesitant?"

"It's what we're *supposed to be training for*. Isn't it? And it's not a world like that. It's . . . people are dying and there's no war. It's quiet when people are dying. If we even had . . . new wells, a way to treat the river water. If we just . . . do you know what I think when I talk to you? I think you've never heard someone having surgery without anaesthetic. I think you've never grown up listening to people die of Cad. How it changes you. Hearing that. Knowing that this was something we used to be able to do — as a society. Relieve suffering. Now it's just you. It's just the universities. Locked away in your little bubbles. Saying, *No, we're not coming out to help. We won't even listen to you scream.*"

"Reid. We can't hear you. It's not like that."

"I know you can't. They made sure of that." I gulp my hot chocolate and burn my tongue, but I feel more awake. Even after seven months, sugar is amazing. I want to tell St. Martin about birch syrup and sugar beets back home and how almost all the sugar ends up going to the hospital for patients who can't eat properly but I also don't want to tell him jack shit. "When I first came here, I asked Jayden where the death board was. And he said *The what?* And it took us like ten minutes to figure out that you don't have one because you have not just days but weeks, months, when no one dies. For us it's every day. So you have to have a live board. And you have to add the names to it. Every day. That's what I left behind. That's what I said I'd go back to. And yes. Now I do know why people don't go back. Because I would love, love to live in a world where I don't have to look at that every day. Because I am almost convinced I can forget that there's a world out there where I once saw it. But you can't un-see what's been seen."

"Yes you can," he says. "I think people can. If they try, if they want it badly enough."

"Well, I don't. It's not a war. It's a massacre. Spectators and speculators aren't helping by watching. That's what you are. We have a . . . we have a live enemy, and you're . . . what? Pretending it's not? It doesn't exist? It's dead, and you can go about your lives not thinking about it? You'd rather it was dead."

"Of course we'd rather have a dead enemy. You're drunk."

"*You're* drunk. I'd rather have a live one so I can make sure I kill it properly. That's the difference between you and me."

"You'll feel differently in three years," he says firmly. "When you graduate. You'll see."

"I won't. Not unless the world changes."

"You. You're the one who'll change. Because everybody does." This time he does get up, and he comes over to sit next to me on the rock, blocking out the faint white light of the street lamp. Behind his head I see an impossible number of stars, clearer than back home, as if we are closer, even though I know that the elevation makes no difference to the human eye.

We're both drunk. Everything seems like a good idea. "I'm not done this conversation," I tell him, and he says, "I know," and we're both mumbling "Well, we probably shouldn't, actually, we've had a few drinks, maybe tomorrow we could talk about it" into one another's mouths. He's not the first boy I've kissed but he's the first boy I've kissed and meant it.

We both keep a death-grip on our mugs, leaving one hand free to either stabilize ourselves on the uneven top of the rock, or touch the other person. I don't care if I fall and I run my fingertips down the side of his face, where the bone is so delicate near the eye, and under his sharp jaw so ferociously shaved before the party, and to the big vein in his neck, thudding so hard it seems to push my hand away.

The alcohol wants me to stay in the moment. The rest of me is speaking the way I used to speak to myself, the way I used to talk to my disease, to the adversary. Maybe the way I win this is by completing this process of shedding. Doing what he says and un-seeing what I've seen in my old life. Only then will I be like them. The gods of Olympus. And at the end of four years then I will say: Now, with all my powers, I will go and help the mortals. If the whole civilized world is contained in this tiny nucleus, this little glowing dome of light in the darkness, then let it be . . . a nucleus. Not a seed. Let it grow crystals that look the same. From here. Spreading out in an orderly circle. Because without my disease I am like this place: I can see what I really am and what I really have the potential to become. I should not throw away this gift. Those who sent me here . . . that's not what they would want either. They wanted me to become this.

Footsteps on the stone ground. We disentangle and I look up, still sober enough to be embarrassed; St. Martin simply slides off the back of the rock and has to pick himself up, shaking spilled hot chocolate off his hands and sleeve. It's Dr. Gibson, of all people — not dressed for a party but normally and soberly in his regular clothing. There is something about his face that seems to see neither of us for several seconds — as if he is looking straight past us to the buildings beyond, to the mountain beyond that, to the sea.

Then he says, "Reid? I apologize for the timing. But you'd better come with me."

I drop my mug and clumsily get to my feet. My head is spinning. I instantly think I shouldn't have stood up, or should have stood up more slowly, but I refuse his proffered arm just as I did when I came. "I can walk," I tell him, shivering. "Where are we going? Am I in trouble again?"

"Just back to the infirmary. There's . . . we've had some communication from your home."

"Communication?"

"About your mother."

Then I am walking quickly with him, almost running, unable to feel my legs. I don't even look back at St. Martin. I am Cinderella fleeing the ball at the stroke of midnight and what I have left behind does not matter.

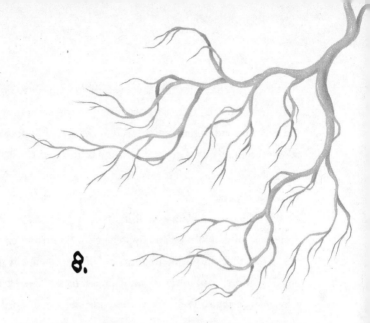

8.

Time slows till I could reach out and touch it passing. Nothing below my shoulders feels like it belongs to me; someone else's hands greatly resembling my own find my old rucksack and begin to pack. I know I'm not thinking straight. I feel feverish again. I don't know how to request travelling food from the kitchen. My canteen is too small but it's all I have. My clothes . . . my clothes . . .

A second set of hands enters the small black-bordered cave of my vision, and I turn to see familiar eyes set in a familiar mask of freckles. Clementine embraces me tightly, and I drop what I have to hold her. She smells like alcohol — her breath, her skin. I must stink of it too. She left the party for me. "I'm so sorry," she says. "You'll get there in time, I know it."

"I hope so. That's all I hope."

"You will."

I love this about her. She says everything with conviction, as if she has been vouchsafed secret knowledge. What will she be at the end of the four years? Not changed, I hope. She takes everything out of my rucksack and begins to pack again, more slowly. I want to put on some music but somehow the silence is better.

My tablet, set to silent as well, lights up now and then with a message of condolence and apprehension. With the party over I had thought people might come by in person, but it's not their way. Even St. Martin only sends a message — albeit a longer one than the others, with a video clip attached. I'll watch it later. I will fall apart at any hint of kindness right now.

"There's a protocol?" Clementine rolls a pair of Howse pants into a tight cylinder and tucks it vertically into the side of the rucksack. "No, you can't take your old stuff. It's full of holes. You'll freeze. I didn't know there was anything like that."

"It's not written down anywhere." I'm shaking again, and I sit on the bed, reaching automatically for the now-cold plate of food I had ordered when I got back to my room. "Dr. Cardinal said ... of course this happens sometimes. I got a letter from ..."

"From your mother."

"No, one of the doctors back home. She was the one who glued me back together enough to leave." My laugh sounds cawing and bitter. "They *do* read your mail here. I knew they did."

"Fucked up," Clementine murmurs.

"So there's Dr. Gibson asking if I want a light sedative? And me going no, I've been drinking some light sedatives. So he asks me how many . . . it doesn't matter. Cardinal says of *course* this happens. It's a large student body and everyone has family. And your mother's Cad is beginning to turn and she might not have much time. So what they do is, they give you two escorts and they blindfold you on the way out and in. What they don't do is take you home. She says I don't have to do exams next week — I can do make-up when I get back. When everyone's off. It's . . ." I'm crying and holding half a sandwich for some reason, and both of these things surprise me.

Clementine takes the sandwich and briskly wipes my face with her sleeve. "You're drunk. Did you consent to all this? Did you sign anything?"

"I don't know. I think so. You do have to sign for the protocol. Because then that's two people that —"

"Two students?"

"Security people. They really. They really don't want people finding them here. Us here, I mean. I don't know what they do to you if you find this place and you're not meant to, but it can't be . . . listen, do you have the Red Flags back home? When someone does something . . . anti-social . . . they're the ones who judge. And decide on a sentence and carry it out. Most people never see them in action. When I came here I started reading up on what the systems used to be like and I thought . . . my God, how barbaric we are back home. How utterly . . . how medieval. Like that. But *these* people, I think, they wouldn't be any different, actually. For something they really cared about."

"You think people might just . . . disappear."

"I don't know. I'm just adding to this mental list of reasons that people don't come back from here. It's as long as *Moby-Dick* by now, this list. Why no one goes back home. This time I'm like . . . what am I bringing back? This idea, like a disease. But by the time I graduate maybe I would bring back . . . only good things. Maybe that's why they insist you do four years without going home. Maybe that's . . ."

"Your mom needs *you*. Not your classes, not your ideas, not whatever. You. You're bringing back good things already."

"No I'm not." But something nudges at my memory and I think: No I'm not. But I *could*.

This is the night that will never end and still the sun is nowhere near rising when I am finally permitted to see Dr. Cardinal again. My watch claims it is three in the morning. Earlier she had seemed sympathetic, though unruffled by the news, with all her edges sanded off like everyone here. Now because I am back and she cannot think of a reason that I am back, I see all her true edges, like stone chips barely peeking out of moss. Those are the ones you cut yourself on when you fall.

"Our building rep is always saying to ask if we need something," I begin, all in a rush. "Because it doesn't occur to people to ask . . . so I'm asking. Whether I can take back the . . . Cad treatment. For my mother. Not for anybody else, I swear. Just for her."

Her face hardens from a kind of benevolent curiosity to first surprise, then anger. Then it is smooth again, as if she has practised this kind of transformation in a mirror. There are so many mirrors here. Back home I barely knew what I looked like. Here, you look always at yourself.

"I'm afraid that's impossible, Reid."

"Why not?"

"Several reasons. First of all, it wouldn't survive the trip. It's thermally and chemically fragile. It needs to be stored at a specific, and very low, temperature and under extremely stringent conditions of pH and salinity to remain active. Anything outside of that range permanently deactivates it. We don't even synthesize a batch here until a student is scheduled for a treatment."

"We could make a —"

She holds up a hand, cold and pointed as ice. "A single dose won't help anyway. And second of all — the reason I didn't want to say out loud, particularly in your condition. Please don't imagine I find this easy to say, Reid. But there is a point in the disease's progression beyond which the treatment has no effect. From Dr. Gagliardi's letter, it is clear that your mother is at that point."

Well, you're the experts, I want to say. I find I cannot speak through the invisible hand that has closed around my throat. Under the fire of her gaze it's as if I can feel the last of the booze burning off, and the hangover beginning. My eyes feel hot and rigid, and it hurts to blink. "What about pain relief then? We don't have that back home."

"We've been told that you do."

"Who said this? Who's passing you all this information about the cities?"

"Reid, I'm going to be blunt. I'm concerned about the uses to which you might put a large amount of strong painkillers in your situation. That's all."

"But I . . ."

"We will not be accessories to murder."

"I . . . what you're saying wouldn't be murder. She's dying anyway. It would be a mercy, it would let her go in peace."

"Please don't raise your voice. I can hear you."

I know what she's imagining. She's imagining me going with a bottle of pills and not doling them out one at a time, but giving them to my mother all at once, if we can feed them to her around the screaming. Cardinal's not wrong. And I'm not wrong either. And it's not murder, it's not. Murder is a very different thing. Murder requires the intent to kill, and I have no such intention. I want a real goodbye with my mother. I want her lucid enough to say goodbye to me. I think of Cardinal's face when we spoke in the botanical gardens that day, us looking at the miracle notebook — I almost want to laugh, remembering what I thought back then, that she was some kind of all-seeing, all-knowing deity.

"You're getting reports from outside these places. But they don't tell you everything, do they? You know what we teach the kids? Starting when they're very little? We teach them which mushrooms can kill you. And we make sure they know where to get them. We teach them: If you're alone when your Cad turns, that's an option. You get to choose whether you take the option or not. It won't be nice and quiet and easy, like going to sleep — it'll be painful and messy and undignified, it'll be three or four hours of agony — but you won't even feel it over what the parasite is doing to you. And it'll be quicker than the days or weeks or months it can take when it turns. It also spares your people from having to watch you suffer help-lessly, or kill you themselves. Imagine that. Can you? Being five years old and being told to memorize exactly how to die? Because it's the best bad option? I just want to give her peace and kindness in those last moments. That's all."

She shakes her head — is that the tiniest trace of horror I see? No, I don't know. Her face is blank and hard as the stone outside. "You should get some rest, Reid. I'll have the escort delayed till tomorrow morning, and you can leave after you've slept and there's good light."

I cannot bring myself to thank her or revile her. I make some vague gesture, and let her assistant show me back out. I feel like I'll never sleep again; I know I'll lie awake thinking of the journey to come, and the nightmare at the end. But how much worse if my mother dies alone. If I am not there. I am all she has left.

Back in our room, Clementine is asleep on my bed, next to my efficiently packed rucksack. I dim the lights and find a plastic packet waiting for me in the kitchen's food slot under a patiently blinking red light. It contains a single round pink pill, no doubt to make me sleep. I put it in my pocket and return to the bedroom with a mug of herbal tea.

Clementine wakes when I sit, although I am being as quiet as I can. Her eyes are bleary with sleep and drink. I should not ask anything of her. And yet there is no one else. How much weight can you put on a friendship when it is new? I have never had to make new friends and so never had to calibrate. What a small life I've led.

I inhale deeply.

"I need to do something they don't want me to do," I say slowly. "And I need for you to not tell anybody. Not even let anybody in the room, if you can."

She yawns. "I won't talk. Whatever it is, I don't want you to worry about that part."

She closes her eyes, opens them again. A flash of light like mirrortalk across the river. "Would they disappear you for it?"

"I don't know. But I have no other choice."

"I got your back," she says. "Somebody's gotta."

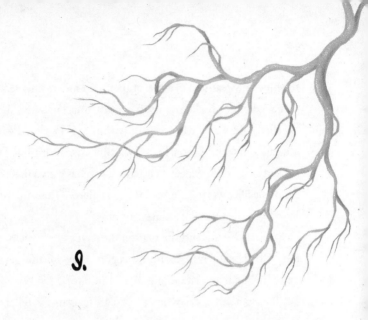

9.

I layer up, mostly by feel. My coat is last, my good wool coat from back home, and my rucksack, tightly packed. I pull the straps taut till it doesn't shift, till it feels like part of my body, the way I did when I came here. Then I cross the room and pull aside the panel that kept us from tripping over my bike every time we went to open the window. The bike carries a faint, animal smell still — my own sweat and blood, the combined dust and resin of the mountains, woodsmoke. Smells that do not belong in this place. Smells from outside. The world.

Clementine says, "So you're not gonna sit and wait for your escort, huh? What *are* you going to do?"

"Better if you don't know."

"But you can't take your bike."

I shake my head, unable to speak for a moment. To leave it behind breaks my heart, but on the walk back from Cardinal's office I ran through my increasingly slim set of options, and the bike only featured in a few of them. If I lose my nerve, I'll be back before she knows it; if I get caught, I'm sure I'll be expelled, and I'll be back to get my things; if I succeed with a clean getaway, I'll be back to wait for my escort; but I've packed as if I don't expect a clean getaway. Basically I'm ready for a specific, worst-case scenario of failure. "This is gonna have to be the official goodbye. For now."

We hug briefly, and she tugs on the straps of my rucksack too. "Good," she says. "Tight. I was gonna say don't forget to write . . . but *don't* write to me. They'll read it."

"No, not here. I'll write to you in Calgary," I tell her. "When you graduate and go home."

"In four years!" She laughs, her voice trembling. "You'll forget me by then."

"Not in a million years."

Last night it smelled like incipient snow despite the clear sky; now the promise is fulfilled, and the air is white. It's not snowing heavily but the flakes are large and wet, and while the air isn't that cold on its own the wind is so strong that my face burns where it is exposed above my scarf. Even the street lights barely penetrate the swirling flurries. Everything is white and grey, grey and white, except for me, in my dark green coat.

I get off the main streets as soon as I can, and in the alleys between buildings I flit past with all speed, hoping I look like nothing more than an unusual weather phenomenon.

Glimpses of books, computers, tanks, vats, piping, cables. Has everyone gone to bed? So few windows give a hint of light. As I run I feel like I am being pushed from behind but I ignore this. I am used to it. The sensation comes from the weight of the past, which I always feel, which they do not.

I'm not heading straight for the infirmary. I'm aiming at one of the storage quonsets, an old one behind the museum. *Desperation* is not the word I want to use here; I just want whatever roiling chemicals that are surging through my body to sharpen me like a knife, make me canny. Partly it is because this may be the last time I get to feel this way, because my Cad will return when I am gone. I know that. I don't want to think about it, about the adversary waking up, hitting the wall of my momentary freedom and joy, scrambling over it. Dragging me to the other side.

I think of the elk, my trophy, his heavy, muscular throat. Head full of daggers. In a spy movie, I would kill anyone who tried to obstruct my mission, but in real life I don't think I could. I think I could not kill if I had to. He could do it, because he is an animal. They all think I am an animal though. Why shouldn't they?

The quonset is dark. I slip to the back of the building, where it faces the mountain, and cast around for a likely shaped stone under the swiftly accumulating snow. All my senses feel ramped up, freshly charged. I have to hurry but I can't rush. There's one: I take off my scarf, wrap the stone in it, and creep to the regular door next to the big ones for equipment and forklifts.

I flagged this place on the map before I even knew what I was doing — what Henryk always called the curse of my memory, which picks things up that you then have to sift through for something useful. Then I didn't think about it again till we began coming here to get supplies for fieldwork — the augers and trowels, bags and boxes they felt didn't need real security, just a home out of the weather. No electronic lock like the newer buildings. It's a regular doorknob with a keyhole, not even a deadbolt.

The storm muffles the sound of my hammering at the knob till its smooth housing comes away, and then I must take off my mittens to pull back the catch inside the round hole. The catch burns my fingers so fiercely that I gasp, panicking that my skin has frozen to the metal, but it hasn't. The relief doesn't last long, and comes with not my first but certainly my strongest moment of doubt: it's colder than I thought. How can I go anywhere in this weather? I should . . . I should stop. Go back to my room. Stay up and read, and in the morning, go with the escort.

No. Stop, I tell myself. Think of Mom. Not of yourself.

Inside, the door carefully shut again, I shuffle through the darkness, coughing. It smells of dust and faintly of mould, slightly sweet, like a rotten apple. I am still holding the stone and I almost laugh: yes, they think I'm a caveman, look at me, slinking around with a rock to bonk someone on the head with. I stoop and put it silently on the floor, and I rewrap my snow-soaked scarf around my neck.

My eyes take a long time to adjust; a little light seeps through the grime-smeared windows at the top of the quonset, smaller than the palm of my hand. All around are boxes and barrels, and one lonely forklift parked in the far corner. For a wild second I wonder if I can steal the forklift on the way back and escape, then dismiss the idea. This isn't a movie.

There. My boot hits what I expected — a barely perceptible bump in the cement floor. Outside the storm wails, snow spattering the metal sides of the hut like thrown stones. I'm not taking my mitten off again, so it's a long struggle to grasp the deliberately low-profile handle and open the trapdoor, first one side then the other. I feel my way down the ladder to the bottom, gasping in the dust.

There are still lots of these back home in Edmonton — tunnels connecting buildings where you can drive a forklift into a small cage that will take it and its cargo up to floor level without having to use precious internal space to have them running around. When this place was designed, I knew the domes would have to have these because they didn't have enough spare land. Back home, they built up, so you could go up. Here, up is mountain, so you build down. All of campus has connections at ground level, but as soon as I spotted this trap door I knew there were more, far more, below.

I wonder who built all this. I can't see the scientists dirtying their hands to chop this out of the stone. They wanted to preserve a present and a future that was beautiful and bright and clean, unlike the rapidly accumulating filth and chaos of the rest of the world.

Later, later. It doesn't matter anyway.

It's a long walk to the infirmary — maybe just eight or ten minutes by forklift. I shiver in the dark, and ball my fists in my mittens to warm my fingers against my palms. If I could see, I would be able to see my breath. The only way to stay warm is to walk quickly, but it's so dark I'm afraid to move past a crawl. I guess the automatic lights respond to the fork-lifts in a way I can't activate, which makes sense. Why would a single person be walking on the tracks?

It's all right. My terror cannot rise any higher than this anyway, light or no.

Storage tubs have been piled over the trap door on the far end, which I had expected. I don't think they're using that quonset on a regular basis any more. But the doors open outwards, so it takes a long time of surreptitiously pushing, nudging, pushing, and nudging again to let me open one door and climb out into a different darkness: clean and sharp, smelling faintly of disinfectant even with the constant draft of the filtered air. This air smells of the present instead of the past.

I need to avoid the patient area, where someone will surely see me. First things first: check the tubs. No medications of any kind. Still, I take off my rucksack and fill the space left with other things we might be able to use at home — plastic boxes of syringes, packs of needles, compressed bags of gloves and masks. Regretfully I leave the thermometers behind — I don't have time to look for batteries and we have none.

Such a simple thing. Still using manual mercury thermometers and after the decades and decades we only have a few of those left. And they are so delicate. When they break . . .

Don't think about it. There's nothing else small I can snatch, so I push the tubs to conceal the open trap door and sneak out of the room into a dark hallway, leaving the door open. If I'm confronted in here I know I can't talk my way out of it, and can only run.

The doors are unlocked on either side of the curving hallway. I feel only a moment of shame: There are no thieves here on campus. Not till me.

Well, they'll lock them after this. I nudge open door after door, hitting the dimmer panel on the walls to keep the lights from coming on at full strength. I see huge machines: X-rays, MRIs, other things. A lab that they must use for diagnostics — I see my reflection move across the face of a transparent cabinet filled with what looks for all the world like cherries but upon closer examination are clear spheres filled with blood.

In my heavy clothing I am sweating again, and the face of the cabinet radiates a welcome cool. And next to it is a grey metal cylinder marked *-80ºC* and plastered with warning stickers but no labels. This could be the Cad cure — part of me so desperately wants the adversary inside me to see it, recoil, give me secret knowledge — but I am already bitterly resigned to the knowledge that it's not a real cure. Only a treatment, as they remind me every four weeks. As I saw for myself when I cut my hand open. Still there. Sleeping dragon. And as cold as it is out there, it still isn't cold enough for this finicky stuff.

No. I have to get something else.

Something on the counter catches my eye. I am at first confused by why it did so, and then I pause and go back. Most likely it's nothing. Most things are nothing. But they so rarely use paper here. Everything is on a screen. Easy to create, easy to delete. Easy to share. You might use paper if you wanted it to be hard to share.

I open the binder and flip through gingerly, conscious of the quiet in here — the hum of the air filter, the faintest rustle of my fingertips against the page. The pages are grimy in the corners, as if this is flicked through just like this, every day. For a moment I feel another flare of hope: instructions for the treatment? True, we don't have all their technology, but if we had the knowledge . . . that would be a project worth throwing the entirety of our campus efforts at. That would be a grand work. What wouldn't we do, what wouldn't we resurrect from the world left behind, if we could do that? By ourselves? And then it wouldn't be trapped here . . .

I should stop when I see the protocol. I already know I should. It's fifty pages long, all dense instructions: this step then this, synthesize this then this. We can't do any of this. I should stop. I should stop reading. I should just . . . take it and go. They can always print a new copy, and I don't have time for this. But I keep flipping through. My heart crawls into my throat and stays there, hanging from its claws, when I see my own name —

The dimmer panel is silent. Light floods the room without warning. I close my eyes reflexively, then try to force them open as I turn, then close them again. I can feel my shirt sticking to my body with sweat both fresh and old and the fabric seems to turn separately from the rest of me. Knew it, knew it, knew it. Knew I'd get caught. I wish I'd gotten caught before this. Before I read any of this. Even the barest part of this — even the parts I don't fully understand I wish I had never seen.

St. Martin thinks you can un-see things. Where did he get that idea?

My face floods slowly with blood; Dr. Gibson's does too, as if he has done something wrong at exactly the same scale and category as I have. What are we both doing in here at four in the morning, blushing? I wait for him to speak first. We teach the kids: First the bear moves. Then you move.

He looks tired — not just up-late tired, but beaten down, tired in his bones. His voice sounds it too. He couldn't go to bed; he expected me to come here. "Reid, please go back to your room."

I'm startled; this is the last thing I expected him to say. It's like when they got me on the way back from my elk hunt — everything quiet, civilized, we're better than that, we don't get violent or loud, we don't get mad. I'm not in trouble but that's also, unfortunately, not my goal. "Dr. Gibson, I asked Dr. Cardinal and she said no, but maybe if you —"

"No."

". . . She talked to you."

"No, she didn't need to. There's only one reason you'd be in here, and I know you think we're not telling you the truth, but it's true: the treatment cannot go with you, and it can't help your mother at this stage of her disease."

I wait. I feel like I've swallowed a mouthful of lava, feel it burning beneath my ribs. I want to be back outside in the blizzard. Back outside in the clean snow. "What if you came with me and —"

"No, Reid. I can't. It's university policy not to interfere with the cities. We take students in. We're very, very careful what we let out."

"I can see that. I see that." In my bitterness the words come out before I mean them to, and not the way I want. "Because you're brainwashing people here, that's why. Not the Howse kids, not *your* kids. Just us. I wondered why you were only inviting students who already had Cad. You know, outside —" Laughter trembles just behind my throat, which shouldn't be possible. He's not smiling. Neither am I. "Outside we thought you had a real cure for Cad. Instead you've got this. Part of a cure. And mind control."

"It's not mind control," he says sharply. It's the first time I've ever heard his voice sound anything other than perfectly level and calm. "Where did that idea come from?"

"It's in here. I just read it. Stop trying to pretend . . . look, right here. *Suggestibility. Easily influenced. It's cumulative.* You used Cad . . . you found the neurotransmitters it was producing that were different from ours —"

"Yes! That's part of how the treatment works."

"— and you weaponized them! It's in here!" I slap the binder closed, and we both flinch. "After four years *of course* no one wants to leave. You're feeding us this . . . constant drip of compliance serum and then you ask us if we want to go or stay like we still have free will. You're creating an army that will just stay put and work for you, perfectly happily, like bees listening to the queen. With no choice."

"We're not. You've completely misinterpreted it. We're studying whether or not there's an association between . . . between this effect you're describing and the Cad treatment shots. We're not *causing* it. And if we do find the association, we'll to correct our formulation to —"

"You did find one. You already knew about it. And you're just . . . going on. That's what changed, wasn't it? The universities are . . . forget the name. Whatever. The fucking domes, you kept yourselves absolutely sealed till you knew this worked and who it would work on. And now you've opened up the tiniest crack so you can keep perfecting it with a constant supply of fresh test subjects."

"Reid, that's not what we're doing."

"What *are* you doing?"

"I just told you. We are working on a permanent cure for this disease. And if we can develop one, we'll —"

"You'll what? You'll send it out into the world? You'll finally start helping people outside the domes? That's it, that's all you were waiting for — to cure the outsiders before you started doing anything else to rebuild the world? Bull-fucking-*shit*. It's been *decades*. You're never going to have a cure because you don't *want* a cure. You want something else."

"I can see you've made up your mind," he says, "but none of that is true. What is true, however, is what you would have seen if you had made it to the back of that dossier."

"I . . . what?"

"There's something unusual about your particular strain of Cad," he says slowly, as if evaluating each word before he allows it to slip out. "It appears to be a genetically distinct subspecies. Not merely a variant — we've seen lots of variants. But it occurred to me to check it when you began telling me about . . . the way you said you've communicated with it. Particularly during your mother's suicide attempt that day. None of that is data. But I was surprised, after sequencing it, that the treatment worked at all. If you stay . . . if we pretend this didn't happen, if you go visit your mother and come back to campus, we could gain a wealth of knowledge from you. You could . . . you could change our entire research program. We both win."

My heart is hammering. I wish people could stop *lying* to me, I wish they could stop using such *trustworthy* voices. I liked Dr. Gibson, I wanted to like him so badly, and now I am studying his face like I can read truth or falsehood written on it and I can't. Am I that valuable to him? To the research? Do I have any leverage here?

"Let me take some painkillers back for her," I say. "Nobody has to know. Like you said: we pretend this didn't happen. I just put them in my bag and when the sun comes up I leave like a good girl. I follow *university policy*. And then I come back and you can study me as much as you want."

"Reid, even if I thought it was a good idea, I can't give you those drugs. They're stringently monitored and tracked; every medication is accounted for. Security knows the moment one pill leaves its packaging, let alone enough to . . . to give you. Without Admin approval, the whole security system will go off like a fire alarm."

"Then no deal." Tears are filling my eyes, despite my best efforts. I want to take it out on him, rage at him specifically — the whole system, the whole university, all of them no matter where they are, they did this. "You'd do it for your mother. You know you would. You're going to hate yourself for the rest of your life for this."

"Please go back to your room. It's your best shot at seeing your mother in t—"

"See her *suffer*!" I shout, unable to stop myself. "See her suffer and die! When I could have helped her!"

He begins to say something else — then he turns, startled, as the door opens and security piles in, three uniformed officers all talking at once through their scarves. *Motion sensors tripped; camera footage in the storage room; items taken; no need for restraints.* For a second I think he's going to tell them to knock it off, let me go back to bed, her mother is sick, she's leaving campus in a few hours, but he quietly confirms that yes, this is the culprit who took the supplies, do what you need to do.

Fucking traitor, I want to yell as they take me back outside, but he meets my eyes for a second, silencing me, and says, "I'll come with you. Just give me a minute to get my coat."

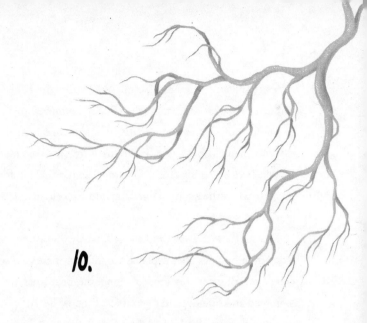

10.

It doesn't really look like a jail cell. Not now that I've seen them in movies. It looks like a hotel room. A futuristic one. Like from that one anime I was watching with Clementine, *Dangerous Admittance*. Guess I'll never find out how it ends. Thoughts orbit my head like seabirds, never landing. I think about what we teach the kids about the animals that share our world: When threatened, there's generally fight, flight, freeze, or appease. Then the human animal can do one more trick: dissociate. We don't tell them that till they're older. That's grade eight stuff. Grade nine.

But of course this university has a jail. Of course it does.

The door looks like the doors in our rooms — white, with a lock on both sides, the glass round and black like an eye. The bed looks about the same. The toilet looks the same. No window. No screens, no tablet. A repurposed dorm room.

Voices outside, one steady, level: "No, it's all right. I already searched her bag for the items she took and removed them."

Dr. Gibson. I open my mouth, as if someone is in here with me, then close it again. He didn't search my bag, much less take back the things I stole. He touched it or held it, for a moment, when the guard nudged me into the cell, so that the door didn't shut on it.

Footsteps move away from the cell, slowly. There's no rush to do anything now. They explained to me that there's a disciplinary meeting for this kind of thing, the board has to be assembled and briefed, and that takes a little while. At least a couple of days, maybe longer, they said. A few days I cannot afford, or I don't know if I can, and that's the problem — not knowing, and maybe missing my mother's last moments because of that. How can they? In the meantime there is enough evidence of property damage to keep me in here. That, I suppose, and my existing record of breaking campus law.

There's a tiny light set into the high ceiling that I cannot reach, and no controls for anything on the walls. There is also, ostentatiously, a camera set into one corner of the ceiling, as big as my head. I glare at it, and sit on the bed, and tuck my fingers into the sleeves of my coat. Outside, the storm rises to a wail that hurts my ears, then quickly subsides. I can feel the speed of the air pressure dropping in my sinuses and my ankles. Never mind escorts or no escorts, what if they just lock me up for the rest of my life because of this?

Some academic career. I want to laugh, and I want it to sound grown-up and sardonic, but nothing comes out. What

I gave up to come here, what the others gave up. An entire life ended in seconds under that boar, nothing but an animal hiding another type of beast — my gross and heavy ambition disguised with hooves and tusks. We teach the kids that you do things together to succeed. Not alone. So I succeeded. And now I am here and alone. And I will return alone, having failed at everything. Everything. No, not everything — Mom will be happy I'm back no matter what.

Well, failed at everything except one thing, then.

I'm not who I was. But I needed who I was to get out of here. And I threw her away. I wanted to be someone new. Congratulations.

I close my eyes and ignore the tears seeping from the lashes. They are tears of rage and humiliation and I should be shedding them. I wish I still had my rock from the quonset. I can't damage anything in here, I don't think, but at least I could entertain myself by throwing it at the camera. It's strange, this is the only place I've ever seen on campus with one of these, I think. There's the broadcast cameras in the classrooms, but never anywhere else. It was almost like being at home, where no one was watching you.

Home. Think of home. This place is not my home. I hoped . . . I don't know what I hoped any more. I was here on their sufferance and they always wanted me gone and now I'm going.

I hunch over and curl into a ball as best I can, feeling winded. I punched myself in the gut, I think. I wonder when they will come back and tell me the meeting is about to start.

I wonder if Dr. Gagliardi has started drugging my mother and how long she can do it for. There is never an excess of the crude poppy tar, and by this time of year, the stored supplies must be running desperately low.

But thinking of Dr. G reminds me of the other Dr. G, Gibson, and why he lied to me in the lab and why he lied just now. I think again: He hardly even touched my bag. How could he be so sure of what's in it or not?

I'm still thinking about it five minutes later when, with an audible crack, the light in the ceiling goes out. The noise is so loud that my body simply throws me off the bed with shock, and then I'm scrambling awkwardly to my feet with my cold limbs sluggishly obeying me. A red light in the camera lens flares angrily but terminally, dying out. For several seconds I simply stand in the middle of the room, hands out in the pitch-dark cell, breathing.

Then I try the door. It's still locked — they must be on a separate circuit.

I already searched her bag.

No you didn't. I dive for it, fumbling, rushing. How long before the power comes back on? Could be seconds. The sealed packets of needles are still there, encased in hard plastic clamshells, each with a little ring of plastic at the bottom to grip it and put it in a syringe. All these things my fingertips have to find in the dark. My only saving grace is that the room is so small.

I withdraw a few needles from the bag. Using only one seems foolhardy. I have a sudden horrible image of the needle breaking and driving itself into my palm. Two will work better, and I can pair them in one of the plastic syringes if I remove the ring. Nerve-wracking when you can't see and have never done it before but needs must. If he wants me to run he should know I want to run too.

There's a nearly imperceptible gap around the plastic housing of the lock and the glass covering — because that's the thing about plastic, they knew it Back Then, they know it now, it has give and flex, it never fits anything exactly perfectly. I jam the twin needles into the gap and then keep pushing, hearing something creak, and then there is a sudden, minuscule crunch. I'm hoping for something dramatic like a spark or a puff of smoke, but the lock simply disengages and the door recedes about an inch into its housing in the wall, letting me see the dark hallway beyond. I have to use my knife for leverage to get it open enough to fully grab it, and then my entire body weight to open the door itself.

Voices in the distance, coming closer. Can I go out the way I came in? I don't think so. I am alone and very exposed in the hallway, panicking and thinking. Juvenile delinquent breaks out of jail and is instantly re-apprehended . . . I'll be twenty in February. I'm not a juvenile delinquent. Just a regular criminal. Think. I haven't broken out of jail. Just my cell.

Up. Quick. Most of the windows are plastic, but the ones that act as solar panels are glass and I saw their dragonfly hue on the way in because they were shaking off the snow. I run to the end of the hallway, find the ramp up, keep running. There is just enough snow-light to show the angled window at the end of the hallway, too high to step over the sill but not too high for someone determined to jump.

Break the glass. How? I hammer at it with my fists, to no avail. Swing at it with my rucksack, but it's too soft. In a minute they'll be on me. The handle of my knife is plastic, but the small area concentrates my frantic swings and the glass stars, but does not break. In a minute, in a minute —

The glass explodes into tiny triangular shards and I duck before I even know what I'm dodging, not registering it till it rolls to a halt on the floor. A rock. Thrown from outside. Icy air and blowing snow fills the hallway a second later, whooshing inwards and then out from the pressure change.

My mittens don't entirely protect my hands as I go up and over the sill, and I've badly misjudged the fall — it's not quite two storeys but it's not ground level either, but I hit and roll and I don't think anything's broken, thanks to the snow. My hands hurt, my eyes burn in the snow and cold, so that for a moment despite the brightness of the blizzard I can't see, and then everything comes back into focus.

Clementine, dressed all in white, holding something dark next to her. My bike. She doesn't come to me; she waits for me to run to her, gasping in the cold.

"How did you know I was in here? Was it Dr. Gibson? Where is he?" I pant, sliding in the fresh snow.

She grabs my arms, pulls me upright. "No damn idea. He just messaged me to say if your bike was still in your room, I should grab it and bring it here. He says I won't get in trouble — he'll take the rap. Absolutely *no* goddamn idea what you're doing but go, go!"

"Wait, he *what*?" Real fear rises up from my stomach, so hot that for a second I think I'm going to vomit. There are no alarms yet but I hear them in my head: he wouldn't have done that if he didn't think something worse was coming. Would he? He took pity on me for a second, he pinged Clementine, and he wants me to get out of here on my own power. That's what he's saying. He isn't speaking to me but I hear him anyway: *Go, get out of here.* Why? What's he afraid of, what does he think will happen to me?

"Is *go* too many words?" Clementine repeats, "Go! Run!"

The map inside my head tells me I am not in a good place to run for the barrier but I still do. I even try riding for a minute but immediately get the wheels fouled in the snow and am pitched off. Not a bad fall, I've had worse, but it still rattles me and all I can do is heft the bike onto my shoulder and trudge through the snow as fast as I can. I cannot waste the chance I have been given.

It is a nightmare of darkness and cold, like all the stars in the sky are frozen and falling, pelting me on their descent, moving at millions of miles an hour. The air burns my lungs till I feel like I'm swallowing blood. The temperature of the air or the running, I'm not sure. Campus life, I think bleakly, has made me soft. That's probably the other other *other* reason no one goes back. Ha ha. Good joke. Who can I tell?

I can't hear anyone pursuing me. All I can hear is the storm, the wind. Maybe it's better if I don't hear them coming. Maybe it would be better to not be warned. At least the adversary sleeps — if I am stopped by anything I will not be stopped by myself. (At least for now. But later, when I miss that next shot . . . no, don't think about it. I can get home before that and then at least I will have people to look after me.)

Home. Home. Just get through the barrier and —

"Stop right there!"

No. I'm so close. I know I am. I won't be able to see the shimmer tonight but I'll know when I hit it and I already know I can go through, that knowledge was hard-won, it is mine alone, not anyone else's, and no matter what happens on the far side of it I will not have to cross it again, not ever again. I am on a one-way journey.

"Reid, stop!"

This time there are hands snatching at me, and I snarl and fight till I am driven to my knees in the snow, disoriented. Which way is up? I have to count the legs to be sure. It's three blue-clad security officers — gasping for breath like I am, I'm sure they do not need to chase many people in their regular jobs — and, to my immense surprise, Dr. Cardinal.

The guards pull me upright and hold me by my arms. I can see nothing of them now except their uniforms — the blue coats, the patches with the *H*, the cold fabric pressing occasionally against my cheek when I struggle. One of them has coffee breath so strong he must have just dropped his cup and run when the alarm went off. I wonder if they are the same guards from before. I didn't look.

"Reid, it's clear that you're very upset," Cardinal begins, but I am done with people speaking to me softly and reasonably, I am just *done*, and if I could have a single prayer granted tonight it would be for her to listen to me just one time before I am excommunicated from this place.

"My mother is dying," I say, because that's the first thing I can think of to say, and then it is not me speaking any more, it is my anger, it is my love, it is my people — the thousands and thousands of them that I abandoned. "My *mother is dying*, Dr. Cardinal, you know that as well as I do, you knew that *before* I did — and this is the kind of world you want us all to live in? The world where I go back and watch her die in agony and come back here, driven both ways like fucking *livestock*, where I come back here an orphan and you study me and I study how to stay in this place, how *best* to not offend anybody so I can live here in luxury forever or, hell, even go to one of the other facilities, even nicer, maybe if I behave myself perfectly for a few decades. Congratulations! You want something wonderful! And I don't! Now *let me go!*"

She stares at me, genuinely stunned. Even in the dim light her face is as pouched and creased with fatigue as mine must be, but I will not wait till daylight for so-called civilized speech, I will not be reasonable, I am going to yell and I am going to swear and if she thinks I'm not going to fight these security guys she's mistaken.

To her credit, she makes one last effort. She motions to the guards to step aside and moves closer to me, her hands out in a gesture both maternal and diplomatic. "We're offering you help to go home," she says. "Let us help you. If you try to travel alone in this, you'll never make it home, and then you'll never see your mother again — that can't possibly be what you want. You're not thinking rationally."

"The only thing that's rational to you is keeping this place's secrets," I snap. "That's the only thing that matters to you. What happens to the students who try to leave on their own? Another secret. And who tries to leave? Nobody but outsiders. Lucky they're the only ones who need Cad treatment, right? The treatment that happens to make people unusually *compliant*?"

Her face goes stony; I've hit the nerve she didn't want me to hit and I regret it immediately. I should not have let her know I knew that. I wonder if this is it, the key to the whole place — that it's the scientists who have this chokehold on administration, not vice-versa. That Dr. Gibson dared stick his neck out even so much as an inch for me, to help me get out of that jail cell if nothing else, because Cardinal needs him. Needs him far more than she needs me. I was merely expendable a second ago and now I have just made myself a *liability*. Why wouldn't they lock me up till my bones turn to dust — or "escort" me off campus and leave me to die with my blindfold still on?

The moment stretches out — and stops when she motions to the guards again. For what little good it will do, I turn to run.

Several things happen at once.

The first is the shrilling howl and vibration of fire alarms — first one, then seemingly dozens. The guards freeze in place, looking around as the buildings light up around us, golden clouds in the blowing snow, and then the exterior strobe-lights start. Almost at the same time my mind begins to form the thought, Is there really a fire?! It seems to be confirmed, with flames as bright as emergency flares in a half-dozen places.

Cardinal and the guards are caught up in the chaos, people filing out of the exits in their pyjamas, still putting on boots and coats, but she hasn't forgotten me, and she reaches for me herself — but we're split up by a surge of people, and not just anyone, but people I *know*, my fellow students, nobody winking knowingly at me, no one murmuring reassurance or next steps, just ferrying me away with surprising speed cross-ways through the crowd, good little worker ants having their first illicit adventure — I know exactly who planned this.

As I run for my bike, splayed in the snow like a dead insect, already losing visibility under the half-inch of white that has drifted over it, I collide with the mastermind himself.

"It's you," I gasp, unable to come up with anything better.

"Clementine messaged me," St. Martin begins, then shakes his head and lifts my bike free, thrusting it at me. "We had to throw this together, basically a few people volunteered to set flares and pull the alarms, and there's another group trying to take down the generators for a minute or two — I have no idea if it'll work. I guess I figure they can't punish all of us. Or maybe they can, who knows."

I'm staring at him, even though I know I should be running — right now, as fast as I can. It's Howse kids and kids from the cities, again people have sacrificed for me, and again

I cannot reciprocate and I cannot thank them and someone else is paying for my mistakes. For a split second I consider asking him to come with me, even though it would be like asking some delicate caged bird to come live with crows in the wild, and as if I've said it out loud, he says, "I would have thrown away a lot of future on you —"

"Shit, I'm glad you can't," I gasp. I'm holding his sleeve for some reason, and under my glove my hand hurts — the scar I got saving him. The scar the mountain gave me. "I'm glad you won't have the chance now. Thank you. All of you. I'll come back, I'll try to come back, and we can . . . we can help . . . look, tell Clementine —"

He's not looking at me any more, tapping something on his watch instead. "Time to run!"

There is no explosion, but it looks as if there should be. The light alone makes me think something should go with it, like thunder after lightning. But as I trudge quickly through the snow, I hear a thrum, or feel it in my bones, my joints, a stuttering sensation instead of the steady hum I would have expected. The crowd cries out as one — in fear or in awe, I can't tell.

They haven't taken down the barrier. But they are disrupting it, and this time when I force my way through the pressure is less, the pain is less. Or perhaps I've gone slightly numb in all the ways that the barrier uses to cause its effects. Either way, no one can hear me screaming into the storm, and then I am through.

Time to run! The storm is unabated out here and I am alone on the mountainside, pausing for just a moment to look back at the lights around where they must have sabotaged the closest generator. A single silhouette pauses, lifts a hand to me. I wave back. They did this for me, they did this together. If you ever succeed at anything you succeed together. Not alone. I never thought them capable of it. Not any of them, not even him. And I will never get to say thank you. The only thing I could do is the thing they cannot do — I, of all people, can find my way back here one day.

I thrust my arm through my bike frame, tug my scarf up over my nose and mouth, and take a deep, knifing breath, looking at the summit. The storm can't last forever. It cannot. And I must be far from here when it ends, if I can.

The chase will begin soon. They'll be expecting me to descend.

I rise.

ACKNOWLEDGEMENTS

I would like to thank my endlessly patient and forgiving agent, Michael Curry, and my brilliant editor Jen Albert, without whose diligence this manuscript would be virtually unread-able. I would also like to acknowledge the beautiful cover by Veronica Park, art direction by Jessica Albert, and copy-editing by Rachel Ironstone. I would also like to gratefully acknowledge the support of the Province of Alberta through the Alberta Foundation for the Arts, its arts funding agency.

PHOTO CREDIT: PREMEE MOHAMED

PREMEE MOHAMED is an Indo-Caribbean scientist and author based in Edmonton, Canada. She completed degrees in Biology and Environmental Conservation at the University of Alberta. She is the author of novels *Beneath the Rising* and *A Broken Darkness* and novellas *The Apple-Tree Throne*, *These Lifeless Things*, *And What Can We Offer You Tonight*, and *The Annual Migration of Clouds*. Her short fiction has appeared in a variety of print and audio venues. Upcoming work can be found at her website, premeemohamed.com.

This book is also available as a Global Certified Accessible™ (GCA) ebook. ECW Press's ebooks are screen reader friendly and are built to meet the needs of those who are unable to read standard print due to blindness, low vision, dyslexia, or a physical disability.

At ECW Press, we want you to enjoy our books in whatever format you like. If you've bought a print copy or an audiobook not purchased with a subscription credit, just send an email to ebook@ecwpress.com and include:

Get the ebook free!*
*proof of purchase required

- the book title
- the name of the store where you purchased it
- a screenshot or picture of your order/receipt number and your name

A real person will respond to your email with your ePub attached. If you prefer to receive the ebook in PDF format, please let us know in your email.

Some restrictions apply. This offer is only valid for books already available in the ePub format. Some ECW Press books do not have an ePub format for us to send you. In those cases, we will let you know if a PDF format is available as an alternative. This offer is only valid for books purchased for personal use. At this time, this program is not offered on school or library copies.

Thank you for supporting an independently owned Canadian publisher with your purchase!